The Last Real Nigga Alive 2

A Novel by Tranay Adams

Kindle Formatting: Renee Lamb

Editor: Ghost

Cover Artist: Sunny Giovanni

Publisher: Tranay Adams

Chapter One

Lafayette lay on his back gripping Montrice's waist as she rode him Cowgirl style. He watched her chunky ass as it slammed into the shaved stubble that was his pubic hairs. He loved to watch his thick chocolate pole disappear and reappear out of his fuck partner's wetness. He clasped his hands behind his head and watched the magic show unfold before his eyes. His cell phone ranged and vibrated, as it danced across his dresser. He slapped Montrice on her ass signaling for her to stop. She stretched her legs out and lay back against Lafayette, grinding her pussy into his manhood. He picked up his cell and saw "California County jail facility" on the screen. A frown emerged on his face and he answered the cell, accepting the collect call.

"Yo?" Lafayette said into the cell.

"I tried to go right, but shit went left."

The caller hung up and Lafayette threw his cell phone across the bedroom into the wall. He looked to Montrice and she was still grinding into him, "Stop, man, damn!"

Montrice rolled her eyes and smacked her lips, hopping off of Lafayette. She picked up her clothes and got dressed. "I'm finna get back home; I don't have time for whatever bullshit you got going on right now."

Lafayette brought a hand down his frowned up face and blew hard, nostrils flaring. He then threw the sheets off of his person and hopped out of bed to get dressed.

***

Batice sat on the couch with Little Gar snuggled up against her watching Cartoon Network. She watched Gar slip off his shirt as he walked into the bathroom. Once she heard the shower water running, she looked to Little Gar who had fallen asleep, playing in his hair and sucking on his bottle. Next, she eased up from the couch and gently laid her son down before sneaking off into the bedroom. She closed the door behind her and approached the Kenwood subwoofer speaker box, turning the box around to expose the hole in it. Seeing the hole, she reached inside and pulled out a few bands secured by rubber-bands. Afterwards, she tossed all of the bands back inside of the speaker box until she was left with one. Once she popped the rubber-band, she counted the dead white men. When she had counted out four big face Benjamin Franklins, she folded it and shoved it inside of her bra. She then placed the rubber-band back around the money and dropped it back inside of the speaker box. Having finished up the task at hand, she placed the speaker box back into its original sitting place. Smacking imaginary dirt from her hands and smiling, she turned around to find Gar standing behind her. Her eyes stretched wide open and her jaw dropped. Little momma could have killed over once she saw her baby daddy standing behind her in a bath towel. He was covered in beads of water and madness was in his eyes.

"I knew I was gone catch your trifling ass clipping me one day." Wrinkles formed around the beginning of his nose and veins bulged at his temples. "What the fuck do you have to say for yourself? What lie are you gone come up with? Go ahead, try your best. I'll wait." He folded his arms across his chest and tapped his foot impatiently.

"I was just getting a few dollars to get Little Gar some milk and pampers."

"Uh uh," Gar shook his head, "Come again, bitch, junior already stocked up, I got my lil' nigga everything he needs."

Batice's eyes shot to their corners as she was trying to think of another lie to tell. She fidgeted with her fingers and twisted the toe of her sandals into the carpet nervously. She opened up her mouth to speak and Gar went on to continue. "Ho, I wish you would fix your mouth to disrespect my intelligence again." Batice grew quiet, trying to think of something convincing to say. All she could hear was her heart beating inside of her ears. She didn't know what her son's father planned to do to her. Little momma swallowed the baseball sized lump inside of her throat and glanced at the dresser. Gar's twin .45s were stashed inside of the top drawer of the dresser he was standing beside. He could grab the both of them and put her to sleep forever.

Gar stalked towards Batice and she slowly backed up until she bumped up against something. Looking from left to right, she realized that she was in a corner. Licking her dry lips, she looked up into her baby daddy's face, terrified. He reached inside her shirt, into her bra, and pulled out the four Big Face Benjamin Franklins she'd just hit his stash for. Gar licked his thumb and counted the money. He then looked up into his baby momma's face and said, "You need four bills to get Lil Gar some milk and pampers? Bitch, you must think I'm fucking stupid!" he smacked her in the face with the money, sending the bills up in the air. The money came raining down slowly to the carpet. "You was gone use my grip to get high off of, wasn't you? Probably with that nigga Theo!" he punched her in the stomach, her eyes bulged and she doubled over. He then brought a left across her head and slammed a right into her chin, dropping her down to all fours on the floor.

A gasping Batice was dazed and could barely crawl forth. She grabbed a hold of Gar's leg and slowly began to pull herself up. "You wanna kill yourself smoking crack and ruin our family? Have Lil Gar out here like he's Oliver Twist and shit? Well, let me help your ass out!" he kicked Batice off of his leg and she fell against the wall, bumping the back of her head. She almost pasted out, but seeing Gar rummaging through his top dresser drawer kept her conscious. She knew exactly what he was going for and she wasn't about to waste another moment inside of that house.

Batice shoved Gar aside as she ran out of the bedroom door. She shot down the hall and went to snatch up Little Gar. Something told her to look over her shoulder. When she did, she saw Gar running up behind her. He wore a hard-face and clutched a .45 in each hand. Batice left Little Gar be and unchained and unlocked the door. She snatched it open and hurried down the steps, baby daddy on her heels. Homie made it out onto the sidewalk and lifted his dual .45s. His fingers pumped the triggers of his weapons and they exploded in unison, sending hot shit in his son's mother's direction. Batice ran down the block shielding her head with her arms. She screamed in terror as she ran for her life, hoping not to catch a hot-one.

Gar lowered his smoking weapons, looking on as Batice hauled ass up the street. His face was screwed up and his chest was heaving up and down. He heard his son hollering inside of the apartment and jogged back into the yard, climbing the steps. He closed the door and laid the warm .45s down on the coffee-table. He scooped Little Gar up into his arms and picked his bottle up from off the floor. He bounced his mini me up and down on his arm as he headed into the kitchen. He turned on the faucet and hot water flowed freely. He held the nipple of the bottle under the water. Once he felt he had cleansed the nipple of germs, he passed it to his son. Little Gar went back to sucking on his bottle and playing in his hair. A grinning Gar kissed him on his chubby cheek and headed back into the living room. When he heard knocking at the door, he just knew that it was the police. He stole a glance through the peephole before unlocking the door and snatching it open. Lafayette crossed the threshold wearing a worried expression on his face. Gar closed the door behind him and he plopped down on the couch.

"Some niggaz were getting live on this block? I heard gunshots on my way over."

Lafayette informed him.

"Nah, not in my section, probably a few blocks over." Gar lied. He noticed the worried expression on his right-hand man's face. He sat on the opposite end of the couch and sat Little Gar beside him. "What happened, my nigga?" he asked.

"Binem snatched up Lil Man. "Lafayette reported, shaking his head sadly. This made Gar sit up.

"It was a botched hit?" he wondered.

Lafayette nodded and said, "Yep. He banged my line a few minutes ago and said 'he tried to go right, but shit went left' before he hung up. The number he was calling from said California County Jail facility."

On his way up the ladder in the underworld, Lafayette had to break a few eggs to make an omelet. His plug at the time, Shameek, had given him a deal on his first brick of cocaine. The offer was too good to pass up, but the only problem was that Lafayette didn't have the money to cop it from him. That's when he and his squad came up with the idea of robbing a brothel. Gar was supposed to have taken up the job, but Lil Man insisted on handling it himself. The job got botched. And although Lil Man managed to escape, he lost his eye in the process. Shortly after leaving the scene of the botched robbery, Lafayette and his niggaz were stopped by two van loads of AK-47s toting Mexicans, working under the orders of Garza, the underboss of the Sanchez Cartel. Come to find out, old Garza was the brother of Isabella, the madam of the brothel that Lil Man had unsuccessfully tried to rob. The cartel snatched Lafayette and his niggaz up and brought them to Garza. He threatened to behead Lafayette and them if they didn't drop a $100,000 dollar bag off in his lap for his sister's pain and suffering. With that, the homies were granted a parting. They managed to get up the money, but they said fuck paying off Garza, they bought some bricks with that shit.

Lafayette got his hood jumping with the drugs that he copped, but with money comes problems. Garza's men snatched up his youngest trap star, Lil Ace, and held him ransom, threatening to hack his little ass up if Lafayette didn't give him $200,000 dollars. Lafayette got the bag to get his little homeboy back, but when he went to go get him, Garza's men brought pieces of him back in separate shopping bags. The sight caused Lafayette to snap. He snatched Garza's gun from off of his hip, shooting him and flat-lining the rest of his men. The under-boss of the Sanchez Cartel managed to escape with his life, but Lafayette found out where he was hospitalized. Lil Man, wanting to prove himself to the squad, took it upon himself to get disguised as a police officer and go to the hospital to finish Garza off.

It was raining the night of the hit and Lil Man dropped the card that had Garza's room number on it. The rain washed off the numbers, but the little nigga thought he could remember them so he carried on with the hit, big mistake. Lil Man got the room numbers mixed up and ended up killing the wrong man. Afterwards, he was apprehended by the police officer that was sent to watch the door. This was how he found himself in the County jail facing a murder charge.

"Man, they got blood," Gar shook his head and ran a hand down his face, blowing hard. "Fuuuuuck! What're we gone do now?"

"Ain't shit we can do but drop some paper for a lawyer for'em, I'll probably try to go see'em."

"You think he'll try to put some shit in the game?" Gar asked whether his brother from another thought Lil Man would snitch on them.

Lafayette shook his head and said, "I can't call it…but if I do decide he needs to be made a memory, you have people behind the walls that'll handle it, right?" he looked to him square in his eyes.

"Man, I got relatives and homies in some of every correctional facility you can name, and they're about that life. But I don't even want to think that way about my homeboy, I'ma keep faith that he gone hold his head."

"All right then. But if push comes to shove, I'ma put the green-light on'em."

"If he's gotta go then he's gotta go." Gar rose from the couch. He dapped up Lafayette and hugged him.

Chapter Two

Theo was laying on the sofa flipping through television channels with his hand shoved down the front of his boxer's. He was dressed in a wife-beater that was yellowing around the neck and tattered jeans. Stopping his channel surfing on Three's Company, he sat the remote control beside his leg and began to watch. After a few minutes he started to nod off to sleep, snoring. Theo shot to his feet, looking alive when he heard someone knocking at his front-door. He rushed to the door, unchaining and unlocking it. He snatched the door open and found Batice's red, glassy eyes before him. Her face was slick with tears.

Theo didn't give a mad ass fuck what she was going through at the moment. All he could think about was getting his next shot of heaven, crack cocaine. "Did you get the money?" he inquired. Batice shook her head no, and wiped her snotty nose with the back of her hand before stepping into the house. Theo closed the door behind her and ducked off into the kitchen. He returned with a glass of faucet water and passed it to her. Batice drunk the water and sat the glass down on the coffee-table.

"Calm down now and tell me what happened." Theo rubbed her back in an attempt to comfort her. He had a fake look of concern across his face.

Batice took a deep breath and went on to tell Theo what had happened between her and Gar. She finished up with, "I just ran and ran and ran! Oh, Theo, I thought he was gone kill me!" she sobbed and he pulled her into him, rubbing her back.

"Man, I'm fiending like a mothafucka. I need me a fix bad." Theo admitted, rubbing her back and bouncing his leg up and down. He did this all the time he was itching to smoke crack.

She pulled away from Theo and said, "Me, too."

"Babe, uh, you tryna do that other thang I talked to you about?" he hesitantly asked her, not knowing what her reaction would be. He had one eye open and his face was squinted to show his teeth. He was ready for her to go ape shit on him for even asking, but surprisingly she nodded her head. "You sure?" he tried to make sure. She nodded yes.

"Yeah, I'm sure. How the fuck else are we gone get high? I needa mothafucking blast bad as a mothafucka right now," Without realizing it, she started scratching underneath her chin, looking like a dog with fleas.

Theo smiled and rubbed his hands together greedily. His girl was willing to sell herself in order for them to get high and he was going to take full advantage of it.

***

"This is all we have left." Gar dropped the duffle bag at the center of the kitchen table before Lafayette. He then sat down at the table, bouncing Little Gar on his knee.

Lafayette unzipped the duffle bag and peered inside. He removed the last two blocks of cocaine they had on deck and sat them on the table, dropping the empty duffle bag beside his foot.

"Two. Two bricks left before we have to press restart and get back out there on them streets looking for another plug." He laid back in the chair and steepled his hands. He blew hard, staring at nothing in particular before looking to Gar. "I gotta think of something, man. With the way this shit is moving these last two keys will be gone in no time. Damn." He clenched his fist and slammed it down on the kitchen table, startling Little Gar. "Sorry about that, nephew." Little Gar looked like he was about to cry until his Daddy tickled his chin and made him laugh.

"Did you holla at Lil Man's lawyer?" Gar inquired, wearing a serious expression.

Lafayette nodded and said, "Lil Man is looking at doing twenty-five years to life, The Boys literally caught him red handed."

"Twenty-five years to life, that's a hard pill to swallow, La."

"I know, man." Lafayette replied before staring into space. He finally took a breath and continued on, "I need to see were dude head is first. I need to look into his eyes and try to feel'em out, you feel me?"

"The homie slipped up and killed the wrong Mexican fool." Gar shook his head sorrowfully. "If he was gone spend the rest of his life behind bars at least let it be behind murking the right mothafucka. Fuck." he swung on the air and jumped to his feet, pacing the floor with his hands on his hips.

"The wrong man, I guess God has a weird sense of humor, huh?

"Two sho'," Gar nodded.

"You heard from yo' baby momma yet?"

"Nah, she's not picking up my calls either. It's been nearly two months and I haven't heard so much as a peep from her. I heard she's out there bad, selling ass to support her habit. Bitch hasn't stopped by to see junior or nothing. On bloods, that crack cocaine is a mothafucka."

"I'm sorry to hear that." Lafayette pounded his fist against his chest, letting his Main Man know that he felt his pain.

"The brazy part is I'm hearing that it's that nigga Theo that's pimping her out."

Lafayette sat up in his chair and said, "For real?"

"Yep, you know what time it is when I catch that fool slipping, right?" Gar looked to Lafayette wearing a dead serious expression and glassy eyes, nose crinkled up. "Homie is living on borrowed time, he just don't know it."

Lafayette nodded his head as he stared ahead at nothing. His eyes shifted to Gar and he spoke, "I'm outta here." He placed both of the blocks of cocaine inside of the duffle bag and zipped it back up. Next, he snatched the duffle bag up from the kitchen table. He dapped up Gar and kissed Little Gar on top of the head, making a beeline for the door.

***

Lafayette and Victoria rode their horses going through the woods, the loud galloping of the horses filling the air as they hurried along. They looked like blurs as they moved hastily through the trees bouncing up and down on the beasts. The crisp dead leaves that had fallen from the trees to the ground made crunching noises as the hooves of their animals trampled them. Victoria beamed brightly as she rode against the wind, her long hair flowing in the air. She looked over her shoulder at Lafayette, who was right behind her. He rode his horse with expertise and that impressed her.

Ten minutes later the queen pin and the hustler made it back to her farm, the bright sun shining on them. They thrashed their leashes and the beasts slowed down to a trot, eventually stopping. After bringing the animals to a stable where they were free to roam, they dismounted them and removed the gear they'd used to ride them, resting them on the fence. Next, they hopped over the fence and made footsteps towards a big white house, which would fit right in on the grounds of a plantation. Victoria pulled off her gloves as she approached the steps of one of many of her estates, a smirk plastered on her lips. She stuffed her gloved into the back pocket of her tan stretch pants. Stopping at the beginning of the steps, she threw her arms around Lafayette's neck and kissed him passionately.

"I had no idea that you knew how to ride like that. Where'd you learn?" she licked her lips and batted her long eyelashes.

"I dug into my repertoire." He angled his head and bit down on his bottom lip, smiling. "You didn't think I was just some hood nigga, did you?"

"No, I knew there was more to you than meets the eye." She kissed him again, their lip locking growing stronger and stronger. His hands slid over the curves of her hips and gripped her bodacious ass, giving himself two palms full.

Lafayette had met Victoria on the same day as Lil Ace's funeral. He went to go get some gas and her limousine had blown a flat. Seeing her bodyguard, Ren, having trouble with jacking up the vehicle with the jack that he had, he offered him his, which enabled him to complete the task. Grateful, Victoria offered to pay him for helping them out, but he refused, asking her out instead. They winded up kicking it one night and it led to sex. Neither of them expected to catch feelings for the other, but, hey, shit happens, right?

Over the past couple of months Lafayette and Victoria had grown closer. They'd gotten to know one another but there were still things that they kept to themselves. Truthfully, Victoria had picked him up to do with as she pleased. He was supposed to be her little boy toy; something to play with until she got bored and found someone else to past her time with. Though that's what she had in mind, her heart had made plans of its own and she winded up catching feelings. No matter how much she tried to deny her emotions, they kept wearing on her until she eventually gave in. She hated to admit it, but she believed that she was falling in love all over again.

Victoria noticed a peculiar look on Lafayette's face. A frown registered on her face and she broke their embrace, holding his hands as she stepped back. "What's up?"

"Huh? What're you talking about?" a line etched across his forehead.

"Something is on your mind?" she caressed the side of his face.

"Nah, I don't know what you're getting at. I'm one thousand."

"No, you're not, did something happen?" she questioned with great concern.

"Nah, nothing like that, I'm just in a bad way right now." Worriment came across his face.

"How so?"

"Look, can I be honest with you without you being judgmental?"

"Of course, I'm not exactly a saint myself."

He blew hard and said, "OK, here goes, I'm a drug dealer. My business is booming, but I'm down to my last two birds. My plug was murdered and I don't know anyone with birds as pure as his, and just as cheap. If I don't come upon another connect then I'll have to start all over again from scratch." He sighed and wiped imaginary sweat from his forehead. It took a lot out of him to tell her that. In fact, he had started not to but

18

he figured what the hell? If she couldn't handle the type of business that he was in then she could kick rocks. "There you go; I put it all out there on the table."

Victoria walked away from Lafayette and his forehead wrinkled. With her back to him, she folded her arms across her chest. She was deathly quiet and seemed to be in deep thought.

"I guess you aren't fucking with a nigga 'cause he's getting his the fast way, huh? It's cool. I understand. Our worlds are just too different." He told her, looking somewhat disappointed. Looking down, he kicked a lone pebble away from him and then looked back up at her. "I'll have Ren drop me back off to my car." He made to leave, but when she called him back, he stopped in his tracks.

"You and I aren't so different, you know?" she started and took a deep breath, her shoulders slumping. "I'm in the same business, only I'm on a different playing field. I deal in cocaine…lots of it. Have you ever heard of Queen Bee? Well, I'm her…she's me. I'm sure you've ran across my stamp at some point and time."

The revelation struck Lafayette like a punch to the gut. He could literally feel the impact of a fist. The nigga couldn't believe his luck; the broad that was supplying Shameek with the bricks he was hitting him off with was standing before him. It really was a small world.

"I…I don't know what to say." Lafayette brought his hand down his fade. He did this every time he was pressed for what to say.

"Say you'll take my secret to the grave with you."

Stopping his hand at the top of his head, he slowly tilted his head up and looked her square in the eye. "I will. I swear it."

"Good. Now, your situation," Victoria took the time to fire up a joint and unleash smoke into the air. "You deal with kilos, right?" he nodded. "Good, 'cause anything lower than that I wouldn't even entertain this conversation. Let's say I shoot you twenty birds at twenty grand a whop? No consignment, I give you the yayo and you give me the loot. How does that sound?" she asked before sucking on the end of her joint and expelling white smoke.

"Deal," He outstretched his hand.

"Unh unh, we'll seal the deal with a kiss."

Lafayette grinned and pulled her close, kissing her deeply.

"Come here. I have something I want to show you." Victoria took his hand and led him up the stairs of her home. She trekked through the living room and stepped before the door of the basement, knocking in a specific pattern. Moments later, she heard the locks coming undid, and then the door was snatched open. Ren stood before them in a blood stained black leather apron and latex gloves. He was clutching a big gun. It looked like it could be pulled out of Robo Cop's leg. It was actually a Desert Eagle .44. His face was screwed up, jaws locked so tight the bone structure could be seen in them. His eyes darted from Victoria to Lafayette and he wondered what he was doing there.

"I'm coming down, step aside." Victoria tapped Ren and he obliged her. She and the hustler made their way down the staircase. Once Ren had locked the door back behind them, he followed them down into the basement.

As soon as Lafayette stepped down onto the basement floor, he saw a naked man hanging from a meat-hook at the center of the room. His body was bloody and bruised. Blood, piss, and shit dripped from his form and onto the black garbage bags that he was suspended above. A frowning Lafayette stood at the bottom of the steps as Victoria approached the bound man. A million thoughts ripped through his mental as he wondered why he was brought down into the basement. Feeling his .9mm being snatched from the small of his back, he whipped around and saw Ren holding it in his hand. The big man pressed a button that ejected the magazine from out of the bottom of the gun. When the magazine clasped to the surface, he kicked it across the basement floor. It hurled across the floor spinning around in circles, looking like a blur and disappearing somewhere within the confines of the shadows. Afterwards, Ren handed the burner back to Lafayette, who looked at it like the useless piece of metal it was without its magazine.

When Lafayette turned back around to Victoria she was standing on the side of the suspended individual. "You see this piece of shit hanging here, Lafayette? He's my husband. I gave this man twenty years of my life and he gave me a broken heart for my troubles." She looked up at the man with tearing eyes and spat in his face. The nasty goo splattered against his face and rolled down his lips, dripping to the floor. "I found out he was off creeping with some young blonde, tricking off the money he made off of the kilos that I gave him. It's all right though, 'cause I left that bitch in the bathtub with her brains floating around in the water. And him, I kept alive, torturing him each and every day; not enough to kill'em though. Nah," she shook her head and sniffled. "I wanted him alive so I could hear'em beg for mercy. Disloyalty is punishable by death, Lafayette," Victoria pulled out the gloves that she stashed in her back pocket and slid them on, flexing her fingers inside of them. Once she was done, she seemed to produce a Glock out of nowhere and pointed it at the naked man's torso, pulling the trigger.

BLOCKA!

A bullet ripped through his abs and he screamed out in agony.

"Raaahhhhhh!" He threw his bloody, swollen face up and looked at Lafayette through his good eye, wailing at the top of his lungs. The hustler could see all of the cavities inside of his mouth, as well as that little thing in the back of his throat. "Fuck you! Fuck you, bitch!" he spat back, red spittle flying everywhere.

"Nah, they'll be no more of that." She scowled heatedly and gritted, aiming her weapon at his knee cap and pulling the trigger once again.

BLOCKA!

Fire ripped through his limb and broke his leg at an awkward angle, leaving his blood pelting the ground. He squeezed his eye shut and clenched his jaws trying to combat the pain, but it was wreaking hell on him, which was why he had tears outlining his eyelashes and rolling down his face.

"Shameek," Lafayette whispered his old plug's name, finally seeing his face out of the shadows.

Shameek had gone missing one day and Lafayette decided to go out to his house in Riverside. He didn't find him home, but his side bitch was there, lying back dead in the tub. The rest of the house had been raided. Lafayette could tell niggaz were there looking for something but they couldn't manage to find it. Remember where Shameek kept his birds stashed, Lafayette took them bitches for himself and continued to feed the streets. He believed that his plug was dead, but unbeknownst to him, Victoria had kidnapped his ass, torturing him for fucking around on her.

"If we're going to go into business, I need to know that I can trust you." Victoria told Lafayette without looking at him. She then took the Glock by its barrel and held it out towards him. "Here! Send one through his fucking skull and put'em out of his misery."

"You do it, bitch, you fucking kill me!" Shameek thrashed around on the meat-hook. "You think you're a fucking man, right? You got balls? Handle yours then!"

"I can't. I know him." Lafayette told her. "He's my old plug."

"Plug or no plug, either you splatter his ass or Ren will be disposing of two bodies instead of one." She swore.

Lafayette hesitantly lifted the Glock and aimed it at his old plug's forehead.

"Go ahead, Lafayette, squeeze." Shameek told him. "Set me free. I'm a hustler, baby boy, I'll find me a plug and setup shop in the afterlife. Where ever I'm at a nigga still gone do it big, ya dig? I'ma be good where ever I go."

"I can't, man." Lafayette told him, squeezing one eye shut and holding his aim on him.

"You can and you will. My time is up and it's your turn to play the game! Now kill me, nigga! Before this bitch kills you!"

"I'm not doing it!" Lafayette contested.

"Lafayette, I'm gonna give you 'til the count of five to shoot this mothafucka!" A very spiteful Victoria pointed up to Shameek. "Or Ren is gonna split your wig." As soon as she said this, Lafayette felt cold metal press against his temple. His eyes shot to their corners and he saw Ren there, holding his Desert Eagle to his dome. The big man wasn't his normal pleasant self at the moment. Nah, his face was solemn and his eyes held the glint of a killer. "One, two, three…"

"Grrrrrrrr." Lafayette scowled and clenched his jaws, causing them to throb. The nigga'z heart beat loud and hard, sounding like the footfalls of a giant. He clutched the banger a little tighter. Suddenly, he turned the gun on Victoria, pointing it right between her eyes and pulling the trigger. The weapon clicked empty and she didn't even flinch. The queen pin stood there for a time before snatching the Glock from out of his hand. "If you gone kill me then kill me, but I ain't 'bouta pop 'em. Nigga gave me the game and put my very first brick in my hands. I'll be damned if I turn around and shoot 'em, when all he's ever done was keep it one thousand with me." He tilted his head downwards and glared up at her, squaring his jaws. The sides of his face throbbed and he clenched his fists, waiting for the bullet that would end his life.

"Aye, La," Shameek called out from where he was.

Lafayette kept eye contact with Victoria and responded, "'Sup, Meek?"

"You always were a stand up nigga, man." He said weakly, eyes hooded and chest leaping up and down, as he breathed heavily.

"Real recognize real, fam."

"Respect."

"Big man," Lafayette addressed Ren. "Gone and handle yo' business."

A smile slowly spread across Victoria's lips and she tucked the gun into the front of her pants. She then applauded the balls of the hustler standing before her.

"I must say, you do show bravery while staring into The Face of Death. I will salute your gangsta, 'cause most in your position would have folded." She looked to Ren and gave him a slight nod. Lafayette knew it was all over then. He shut his eyes and waited for it to be over.

BLAM!

Lafayette's eyes peeled open and his forehead etched with creases, he couldn't believe that he was still alive. He looked to Victoria and then to Shameek. As soon as he turned his head to him, bullets came back to back, tatting up his torso. The kingpin took his last breath and his entire body went slack on the hook. His blood fell rapidly and pelted the surface below.

Lafayette shut his eyes briefly and crossed himself in the sign of the crucifix.

Ren lowered his Desert Eagle from the back of his skull.

"Now what?" Lafayette asked Victoria.

"We go on to do business." She responded.

Victoria Couture was the daughter of Haitian immigrants, Duran and Henrietta, a kingpin and his wife. In the 1970s her father went to war to defend his empire against his best friend, Sharone. Sharone was his underboss. He'd gotten sick and tired of answering to him. He wanted to be top dawg and he felt like the only way for him to be it was to take out Duran. Now, although Sharone was outgunned, he was smart enough to know that it wasn't how many people you shot but who you shot. With that in mind, he had one of his hands attach an explosive to the warring parties' limousine. The device was rigged to explode as soon as its driver turned the key in the ignition. Victoria's mother and father lost their lives in the blast, but luck was on her side. She was going to get a ride to school that day but she'd forgotten her backpack inside of the house. When she ran back to get it, the entire garage burst into flames, sending burning body parts flying everywhere.

With the deaths of the Couture's Sharone thought that he was next to helm the throne, but he'd forgotten about Duran's brother, Larenz aka Ren. Ren brought it to Sharone's entire clique, wiping out all of them fuck-niggaz and leaving their leader alive for his niece to do away with.

FLASH BACK

"Vickiiieee." Ren called out over his shoulder to his niece. She took her time coming down the steps, sliding her hand along the guard rail as she went. Once she reached the landing, she went to stand beside her uncle. He kissed the top of her head and rubbed her back lovingly. Afterwards, he turned his eyes in Sharone's direction and pointed his Glock .50 at him. "You see this bitch ass nigga here, Baby girl?" she nodded yes. "Well, thisthe mothafucka that murdered your mother and father." Hearing this, Victoria looked alive. She looked from her uncle to the nigga gagged and tied to the iron chair.

A wide eyed Sharone looked from Ren to the little girl, trembling. Wet expanded at the crotch of his slack and dripped onto the floor between his leather alligator shoes. From where he was perched, the girl and her uncle looked like silhouettes with the basement lights shining on their backs. The only thing he could make out about them were their waists on down. This made them appear mysterious and creepy to him.

"Now, I could gone and smoke 'em for you, but I thought that you'd want to do the honors, seeing as how he was the one that capped your parents."

"I wanna kill 'em, uncle." She looked to her father's brother, tears sliding down her cheeks.

"All right, Baby girl, he's all yours. Now, have you ever shot a gun before?" he asked her as she wiped her face with the back of her fist, sniffling. Little momma shook her head no. "It's okay. I'll help you." He stepped behind her and kneeled down, placing his Glock into her hands and aiming it at Sharone. The nigga went wild in his chair screaming and rocking back in forth in the chair. Suddenly, he stopped moving and threw his head back sobbing and begging for his pathetic life. His shoulders shuddered hard and his entire form quivered. "Hold it just like that, Baby girl." Ren stood erect and walked over towards Sharone, his shadow casted on the floor and shading him. He waltz right up and smacked fire out of that hoe ass nigga. "Man the fuck up, nigga! All the niggaz you done had peeled. Now it's your turn and you shaking like you wearing a G-string and stilettos! Take it like

a fucking man!" Smack! He smacked him a second time, leaving red hand imprints on both of his cheeks. He then walked back over to his brother's daughter, leaving homeboy wailing in his chair and pissing on himself. Ren kneeled back to the surface behind his niece, helping her aim his gun. He whispered instructions into her ear. She shut one eye and licked her lips, having found the area on her target she wanted to hit. Abruptly, she pulled the trigger twice and put two into Sharone's heart. The weapon wafted with smoke and Ren brought it up a little higher. "Now, for the kill-shot, you got it lined up like I told you?" she nodded yes and slowly pulled back on the trigger. The back of Sharone's head exploded, sending pieces of his skull and brain fragments smacking up against the black garbage bags that covered the wall and floor surrounding him.

After murdering Sharone Victoria broke down crying. Ren took the Glock away from her and got down on his knees, embracing her. He held her in his arms as she cried her eyes out, staining the breast of his button-down shirt. He rubbed his hand up and down her back soothingly and talked to her in a calming voice.

"It's okay, Baby girl, let it all out, let it alllll out." He told her.

Ren ran his brother's empire and groomed Victoria to be his successor. When the day finally came, he stepped down and assumed the position of her bodyguard and mentor.

PRESENT

"Do business? Me and you?" Lafayette looked at Victoria like he couldn't believe her, motioning a finger between the two of them.

"Yes. You and I." she grinned.

"What the fuck was all of this for then?" he pointed to Shameek's lifeless body.

"A test." She held her wrists behind her back. "I needed to know that you were loyal. You not going through with killing my bitch ass husband proved that."

"What if I had killed him?"

"Then you'd be lying at my feet, handsome." She smirked and caressed the side of his face, like what she'd just said wasn't a big deal.

Lafayette took a deep breath and exhaled, thankful that he always stuck to the codes and principals that he lived by.

"You're gonna do alright in this business, kid." Ren smiled and patted him on the back.

Chapter Three

Lafayette's thoughts ripped through his mind as he pushed his rental through the streets. It was true what they say about hell having no fury like a woman scorned. He had witnessed it firsthand. Victoria had Shameek hanging in the basement of her farm house like half of a slab of a pig and had been torturing him for the past couple of weeks. If that wasn't enough, she had her bodyguard air his ass out.

Lafayette hated to see the O.G get done like that. He had always shown him love. Shameek was a pretty solid dude, but his time in the game was up. Lafayette couldn't help thinking that everything that had led up to that point had been in God's plan. That maybe Shameek had to be taken out of the game so that he could rise to power and take his place. If this was the case then Lafayette was going to make sure he filled that spot, like the perfect piece to a puzzle.

Lafayette was going to be mindful of Victoria too. She went to work on Shameek behind his infidelity, which showed she was a wicked bitch when she felt she had been wronged. He could tell that she had caught feelings for him. She'd started to play him close like he was her nigga or some shit.

Who's to say that she wouldn't catch a beef with him if she caught him out in the streets with another broad? If she flipped out on him he could be the next nigga hanging from a meathook down in the basement of her farm house.

Nah, fuck that. I ain't going out like that. Bitch send some niggaz for my head then I'ma take a couple of they asses with me.

Lafayette pulled upon the block just in time to see his Main Man emerging from the liquor store, drinking a quarter juice. Once he saw him wrap up a conversation he was having with a crackhead, he waved him over.

***

Gar emerged out of the liquor store drinking a quarter juice. He had just brought the bottle down from his lips and wiped his mouth with the back of his hand, seeing a crackhead approaching him.

"My nigga, does it look like I'm slinging to you?" Gar said to the crackhead trying to cop from him. "Take that shit back to the hood, bruh." He shooed the fiend away and watched him hustle his way across the street. Gar grinned and shook his head, thinking that the poor bastard was running along to catch a one way ticket to death.

That crack is a mothafucka, boy.

Seeing Lafayette, Gar walked over to his ride and kneeled down inside of the passenger side window. "What's up?"

"We back on, I gotta new plug." Lafayette smiled.

"Yeah?" Gar grinned.

"Yeah. We're back on, my nigga. Niggaz is gone be straight."

"Cool. A nigga was low ball worried for a minute. I thought I was gone have to start masking up and running up in niggaz shit."

Lafayette laughed. "Nah, fam, we're straight like six o'clock. We're about to receive the biggest shipment we've ever dealt with."

"That's what's up."

"Well, look, I'ma go ahead and take it in. I'll get up with chu." he dapped Gar up and drove off.

The next day

Chill ripped down the 110 freeway in his black X5. He spat the lyric's to ASAP Rocky's *Fuckin' Problem* as it blasted through the speakers. He gripped the steering-wheel with one hand while his freehand rested on the back of the shaved head of the voluptuous chick that was sucking his dick. The slurping sounds that she made were drowned out by the blaring music. Suddenly, Chill stopped rapping and his eyes began to twitch and then flutter. He could feel the semen building up in his loins. He moaned like a walking dead man and licked his lips, sliding down in the driver seat. Shaved head's mouth felt like warm, wet silk against the sensitive skin of his member. Chill's hand slipped below shaved head's head and grasped the back of her neck, giving it a slight squeeze. The harder she sucked his meat, the tighter he squeezed the back of her neck. The pressure to the back of the woman's neck coupled with his groans of pleasure let her know that she had a head game that was off the chain. Shaved head squeezed his meat and jacked it, as she bobbed up and down his grown man.

Chill's eyes flickered white. He bit down on his bottom lip and clawed at the leather passenger seat. When he felt himself about to shoot his male mayonnaise, he pushed the woman's head down causing her mouth to take in two more inches of his throbbing manhood. With two violent jerks he shot his load deep down the woman's esophagus. When she tried to lift her head, he held it in place and made sure he released every last drop of his warm semen. Shaved head came up adjusting her enormous Dior shades and giggling, licking his sperm from the corner of her mouth. She let down the sun-visor and looked into the rectangle shaped mirror. She wiped her mouth with her fingers and applied another coat of M.A.C lip-gloss.

She capped the lip-gloss and dropped it into her designer handbag.

"Damn, lil momma, you got talent. Whoo," Chill smiled, looking down at his glistening dick. "Look into that glove-box and hand me a couple napkins." He took the napkins from shaved head and he wiped his cock off. Once he was done, he balled the napkins up and threw it out of the window. He looked over at shaved head as she searched through her handbag. She had a face only a mother could love, but her body was insane. She had tits the size of cantaloupes and a booty that made you want to scream. From the neck down she was the shit.

Staring at shaved head made Chill's dick hard all over again, he licked his top lip and bit down on his bottom one as he molested her with his eyes. He couldn't wait to see what the inside of her felt like.

Shaved head slipped a stick of Winter Fresh gum into her mouth. She turned her eyes on Chill as she chewed on it. "So, where are we going to eat?" she asked.

"Ummm," he snapped his fingers trying to recall her name, but couldn't remember it. "I'm sorry, sweetheart, what was your name again?"

Shaved head grinned. "It's Jaquoia."

"My bad, baby, a nigga got short term memory loss and shit, I smoke too much Loud. Matter of fact," Chill opened up the glove-box and pulled out a half an ounce of O.G Kush. He dropped the Ziploc of pretty bright green buds into her lap and said, "Roll that up for me. I gotta pick up these lil sixty bands right quick. Afterwards, we can eat where ever you want."

Since Jaquoia had met Chill he'd been bragging about how he ran Los Angeles. She'd fooled around with plenty of dudes that claimed to be balling and shot calling, but in the end it came to light that they were fronting. Chill seemed to be different though. He'd been spending money like it was running from a faucet since she'd met him. They'd dined at the finest restaurants, guzzled champagne as if it were water, went on shopping sprees and made it rain in strip clubs. As far as she could see Chill was the genuine article. Either that,or he had a throng of women that were papered up. Either way he had access to an obscene amount of money and she wanted her stake in it.

Chill pulled up in front of a shabby looking house with a rusty iron fence. He killed the engine and turned to Jaquoia, gripping her thigh.

"I'll be right back." He hopped out of the truck and jogged into the yard.

Jaquoia settled down in her seat, chewing her gum and inspecting her manicured nails. Seeing a flicker of movement in her peripherals she looked up and saw a dread headed homeless man. His locks were filthy and tangled; they looked as if they were infested with cob webs and spiders. He was in a tattered jacket, wool brown gloves and tattered baggy blue jeans. The homeless man sprayed the windshield with Windex and began wiping it with a balled up news paper. Jaquoia went to rant and rave when she heard Chill approaching.

"Aye, get the fuck away from my whip!" Chill hollered at the homeless man as he approached with a hard-face. He had a backpack slung over his shoulder and his thumb was hung in the loop of his crimson red jeans. "Gone, man," he shoved the homeless man, causing him to stagger back, fear in his eyes. "Get the fuck on!" he shoved the man again and he dropped the bottle of Windex. The homeless man reached down to pick up the Windex and came back up holding a black .357 Magnum revolver. Seeing the revolver caused Chill to panic. He went to draw his banger, but the homeless man pressed his weapon under his chin. The coldness of the barrel caused Chill to stiffen and swallow the lump that had formed in his throat.

"I wish a nigga would." Zay eye-fucked Chill as the corner of his lip twitched. He held out his freehand and flexed his fingers. "Un-ass that burner…nice and slow, like." Chill reached into his waistline and pulled his banger. He slowly outstretched his hand to give Zay the banger. As soon as Zay's hand touched the gun, with lightening fast reflexes, Chill pulled a second one from his waistline. He raised his heat. He was about to pull its trigger, but a slug caught him in the shoulder and threw him off balance. He crashed to the asphalt howling in pain as he bled.

Zay looked over his shoulder and saw La'Chat hop out from the passenger seat of the X5. A Louie Vuitton scarf covered the lower half of her face, leaving a pair of intimidating eyes exposed. She started in Chill's direction with her hand curled around the handle of a smoking Desert Eagle. Zay's head whipped back around to Chill, catching him reaching for the second gun he'd pulled. He quickly kicked the joint out of his reach, sending it spinning in circles across the ground. He then pressed his raggedy sneaker into Chill's wounded shoulder and mashed on it, causing him to holler out in excruciation. Zay's face twitched with anger as he shot daggers at his victim. He aimed his revolver at the center of his forehead and applied pressure to the trigger but La'Chat grabbed his wrist.

"No! I know there's plenty more scratch than where that came from." She said. "I know this nigga gotta safe somewhere, I wanna crack this piggy bank for all it's worth." Zay

40

nodded in agreement. "Snatch'em up and toss'em in the trunk," she set her sights on Chill, mad dogging him before stomping down on his stomach. He hollered out and hugged his stomach, wincing. La'Chat then slung his backpack over her shoulder and walked off. Zay threw Chill over his shoulder and carried him off to the X5.

***

Lafayette sat on the stool waiting for Lil Man to come through the visiting room door. He looked from left to right and saw that the stools on both sides of him were occupied. The visitors were on the telephone talking to their loved ones. He glanced at his G-Shock, and when he looked back up he spotted Lil Man. He was in a jumpsuit and it was fitting tight on his muscular form. His body was ripped with muscles. He'd always been a muscular dude, but now it really showed. His short natural was now in ten neat cornrows that reached just past his ears. He wore an eye-patch and scruffy facial hair. A smile stretched across his face, happy to see Lafayette.

Lil Man planted his ass on the stool and snatched up the telephone. Lafayette was right behind him, placing the receiver to his ear.

"What's up, Lil? You done got big ass shit, nigga! Fuck you been doing in here?" Lafayette took note of Lil Man's physique. The little nigga smiled and his pecks did a little dance.

"I've been busting down these ghetto workouts, family. You know they don't have weights inside this shit-hole. You gotta make due with what chu got."

"I heard that." Lafayette agreed. "So did Goldberg come see you?"

Lil Man licked his lips and nodded. "Yeah, he came through yesterday and got at me. They're talking twenty-five years to life. He said he's gonna try to get me fifteen though."

Lafayette studied the little dude's eyes, looking for signs of wavering loyalty. Lil Man's eyes didn't betray what he felt inside of his heart. Though he did sport strands of gray hair throughout his cornrows and his scruffy facial hair, that was expected; he was facing life in imprisonment. What man wouldn't be showing signs of stress being under that amount of pressure?

"All I can do is take this shit on the chin. I've done bids before...not this long of course. But a nigga done made his bed and now he's gotta lie in the mothafucka. This is the life I chose, and now I've gotta own up to it, feel me? It's called T.Y.C, Take Your Charge." Lil Man stared Lafayette directly in his eyes. He knew Lafayette was there to read him and see if he was going to rat or not. This little conversation of theirs was to determine if he would get a death sentence or a pass. He believed Lafayette was shook and he couldn't blame him, because if he was in his shoes he'd be the same way. Lil Man had enough knowledge on Lafayette's operation to sink his entire organization. All he had to do was cooperate with the D.A and he could get his time cut significantly.

"I know you wouldn't rat, 'cause that's not how my niggaz built. My niggaz are stand up. We're rare. Young dudes that still adhere to an old school code." Lafayette matched Lil Man's stare. "I love you, my nigga." He placed his fist against the Plexiglas.

Lil Man placed his fist against the Plexiglas against Lafayette's fist. "I love you too, La."

There was a silence between the two men as they stared into each other's eyes. Suddenly, Lafayette hung up the telephone and shot to his feet. Lil Man hung up the telephone and watched Lafayette's back as he made his way out of the visiting room.

Only time would tell if Lafayette made the right call or not.

***

Chill's eye was swollen shut and he had a big lump on his forehead. Small red streams flowed from his nostrils and over the strip of duct-tape that sealed his mouth shut. His shoulder was wrapped in duct-tape to slow its bleeding. He sat at the center of the living room floor of his baby mansion, bonded to a chair by duct-tape. He thrashed around in the chair trying to break free, but the duct-tape held fast. Realizing that his efforts were futile, he settled down in his seat, breathing heavily. His head darted around the room trying to see where his kidnappers were. Though Zay and La'Chat were out of sight, he could hear them rummaging around somewhere inside of the house. Suddenly, the sounds of the bandits rummaging fell silent. Then there were footfalls that grew louder and louder at Chill's left. He looked to where the noise was occurring from and saw Zay hustling down the staircase with a pillowcase. Hearing footfalls coming from his right, Chill looked and La' Chat was approaching from the kitchen, taking a bite out of a pear.

"You sure don't have much to eat in here." She said to Chill, and then looked to Zay. "What did he have up there, Bae?"

"My man didn't have shit up there, but a measly forty grand." A frowning Zay slapped Chill upside the head hard as fuck. He then snatched the duct-tape from his lips and kneeled down, looking into the windows of his soul. Zay's eyes were glassy and insanity was hidden behind them when he spoke. "Check this out, homes, I know you got more than them few lil dollars around here. You gone tell me where the mother lode is, 'cause if you don't, I'm gonna take the butt of this here piece of mine," he held up his .357 Magnum revolver, "and I'm gonna crush your testicles into wine. Now, do we understand one another?" he looked him square in the eyes and his nostrils flared.

Hearing the plan Zay had for his nuts caused Chill to cringe. Tilting his head back, he shut his eyes briefly and swallowed the lump of fear in his throat. Though the muscle headed brute hadn't laid a hand on him, he could actually feel his balls being crushed under the weight of Zay's trusty revolver. Chill had close to a million dollars stashed in the house he'd set his wife and his new born son up in. But he couldn't take Zay and La'Chat there and risk harm coming to his family.

Chill made up his mind to suffer through whatever torture the big man and his better half could dish out. There wasn't any way in hell that he was giving up that sensitive information. He didn't want to have to face the repercussions for his refusing to cooperate. So he knew he had to think of something fast if he was going to save himself from a world of hurt and his family the heartache of having to make funeral arrangements.

"What's it gonna be, big dawg?" Zay asked, pulling Chill away from his thoughts. The big time hustler looked up at the man that literally held his life in his hands.

"Listen, all my money is tied up in the streets, I don't have no more than a couple of cars and some punk ass jewelry." Chill lied through his fucking teeth. "But I do know a nigga that's handling. I'm talking big weight, this nigga moving a hundred bricks a month."

Zay and La'Chat exchanged glances and cracked slight grins. The big man looked back to Chill and asked, "Who is this cat we're talking about?"

"Lafayette."

Zay and La'Chat both frowned. "Lafayette? Where is he from?"

"Dude is from the eastside. The Low Bottoms."

"Well, I'll be damned," Zay looked to La'Chat, "That lil black son of a bitch. To think a Big Willie was right up under our noses this entire time."

"Are you thinking what I'm thinking, babe?" La'Chat smiled wickedly.

"Yep, we're hitting Lafayette's ass."

"Sho' ya right." La'Chat held her pear up to Zay and he took a bite out of it.

"So are y'all gone let me go?" Chill looked from La' Chat to her man.

Zay finished scoffing down the pear and wiped his mouth with his coat's sleeve, turning to Chill. He nodded and said, "Sure…to hell." Homeboy opened his mouth to scream but before he could a bullet ripped through his torso. The impact from the bullet tilted the chair back and he went crashing to the floor. He lay there groaning in agony and squirming around, wincing and gritting. He squeezed his eyes shut to combat the fire spreading in his center.

Zay observed him for a moment, angling his head. He watched as he blinked his eyes and blood bubbles formed inside of his grill, rolling down the corners of his mouth. The big man didn't stay to watch his victim's final moments. Instead, he tapped La' Chat and they made his way for the door.

Chill died that day leaving his wife a widow and his child fatherless.

Chapter Four

The next morning

Gar stirred awoke hearing knocks at his door. He had scum in his eyes and dry spit at the corners of his mouth. He looked to his left and found his fuck-buddy from the night before lying on her stomach. She was naked and her long hair was sprawled all over the pillow.

Gar looked to the digital clock on his nightstand. He then picked up his cell phone and glanced at the screen. He had six missed calls, four voice mails, and three text messages. His cellular rang with a new text message. It was from Lafayette. He read it and it said *Open the door, nigga. We have business we need to tend to.* It dawned on him that he was supposed to roll out with his Main Man to pick up the birds that morning. He shot to his feet and darted out of the bedroom. He took a quick glance through the peephole. Once he confirmed that it was Lafayette, he unlocked and unchained the door before snatching it open.

"Goddamn, nigga, fuck were you in here doing?" Lafayette asked as he crossed the threshold, looking the house over.

"I was K.O'd. It was a long night, my nigga." Gar stretched and yawned, causing his bones to crack and readjust.

"I see." He spotted a cluster of empty liquor bottles and cups on the coffee-table. He pulled his .9mm from the small of his back before plopping down on the couch.

Gar fished through the ashtray on the coffee-table until he found the roach end of a blunt. He picked it up and put fire to the end of it with his lighter. He took a few drags and blew out white smoke.

"Let me get this bitch up outta here so I can get dressed." He said, disappearing into his bedroom.

Lafayette heard a loud smack and then a woman yell "ouch." He assumed that Gar had smacked whoever he had inside of his bedroom on the ass. He then heard Gar say "It's time to go, I got shit I gotta do. Get cha shit together. Hurry up!" A moment later, Gar's unruly ass emerged from his bedroom pulling his fuck-buddy along by the arm, leading her towards the door. The strap of her dress was hanging off of one of her shoulders and she was carrying her high heels in one hand. Gar was pulling her along so fast that she nearly tripped and fell.

Gar snatched open the front-door and shoved his fuck-buddy out. He was just about to pull the door closed when she grabbed it.

"Wait a minute, how am I supposed to get home?" she asked. "You've gotta at least gimmie some money to catch an Uber."

Gar fished around inside the pocket of his Dickie's and produced a few balled up bills. He snatched the girl's hand and smacked the bills into her palm, balling it closed. The girl un-balled her hand and straightened the bills out. She frowned up when she saw exactly how much money he'd given her.

"Three dollars? The fuck am I supposed to get back to West L.A with three funky ass singles?" she placed her hand on her hip and switched the weight from her left foot to her right foot.

"Catch the bus!" Gar slammed the door in her face and bopped to his bedroom to get dressed.

Lafayette smiled and shook his head. He then picked up the remote control and turned on the flat-screen television set.

***

Gar was posted up beside Ren inside of an old warehouse, watching the handlers load the blocks of cocaine inside of the back of the U-haul truck. The cocaine was hidden inside different furniture pieces like vases, lamps, box television sets, couch cushions, etc. Lafayette had brought Gar along for the ride so he could watch the handlers every move and make sure that there wasn't any funny business. After today Gar was to meet with Ren to pick up the shipments. As active lieutenant in Lafayette's operation this was to be one of his jobs.

"Shit!" Gar cursed and threw his Bic lighter to the ground. He couldn't get it to produce a decent flame to light his L for shit. He turned to Ren, blunt dangling from the corner of his mouth. "You think I can bum a light off you?" Ren reached into his pocket and produced a Zippo-lighter. After he sparked up Gar's blunt, he snapped the lighter closed and shoved it back into his pocket.

Gar took a couple drags from his blunt before blowing out a roar of white smoke. He tried to pass it back to Ren but he waved him off. While smoking his L, Gar took in Ren's physique, sizing him up as his attention was focused on the handlers. "Youz a big mothafucka, Blood. What chu used to play? Football or something?"

"Nah, I used to wrestle back in high school," Ren admitted without taking his eyes off the handlers. "I would have gone pro, but a car accident stole that dream. I broke both of my legs."

"Ouch." Gar cringed, imagining how painful that must have been. "How much do you lift? 'Bout three hundred?"

Ren finally took his eyes off the handlers and looked to him. "Three fifty." He grinned and made his pecks jump, one at a time.

"Yeah, it's safe to say I wouldn't shoot chu a fair one, I'd have to blast your big ass." Gar stated jokingly but serious.

They both laughed.

***

Lafayette and Victoria lounged on the couch in the living room of the farm house, sipping champagne and shooting the shit.

"Your friend Gar…How long have you known him?" Victoria asked.

"I've known Gar for a minute. That's been my Ace since, like, forever."

"Is it safe to say that you trust him with your life?" she took a sip of champagne and watched his expression as he replied.

"Yes."

"More than you trust that other friend of yours, Lil Man?"

Lafayette blew hard and licked his lips. "I grew up and threw up with Gar. I feel like I know him inside and out. I'll never question his loyalty to me." He took the time to gather his thoughts. "Lil Man has been a stalwart soldier, but I can't say I know him as well as I know my Main Man."

"Let me ask you this," Victoria began. "If it was your Main Man behind those walls would you still find yourself with this same dilemma?"

"No. And as foolish as it sounds, I'd be willing to bet my freedom and my life on Gar in that same situation."

"Good, that means you're vouching for him. He knows who I am now. If he was to ever show shade we'd both land behind bars. Should that day come, I want chu to know that I won't hesitate for a second to crush the both of you. Do we understand each other?" she turned around and looked him square in the eyes.

"Are you threatening me?" Lafayette's eyebrows arched and he clenched his jaws.

"No, I'm promising you." she caressed the side of his face and kissed him, tenderly. She then walked over to the living room table and sat her flute down. "Now, this other matter you brought to my attention." She walked around the rich white grand piano, allowing her finger to trace its edges. Her reflection was cast on the floor.

"Garza and Isabella Sanchez, I need them gone like yesterday." He answered before taking a sip of champagne.

"Garza Sanchez. He's connected. His brother is head of one of the most ruthless cartels in Mexico." She informed him.

"I know. Is that going to be a problem?"

"Not at all; if I take care of him, I'll also have to do away with his brother." She relayed. "He's a business associate of mine; I can get close to him. So having him touched wouldn't be a problem."

Lafayette blew a sigh of relief after hearing Victoria could handle his problem so easily. He was glad he had hooked up with her. It paid to know people in high places.

"Boy, I tell you, you just lifted some weight from off of my shoulders. I don't know how I could ever repay you."

"I've grown quite fond of you, Lafayette. And I'd like to think that the feeling was mutual." She smiled.

"Then your thoughts would have served you correct." He smiled and winked at her, taking a sip of champagne.

"Well, how about we spend the night together once you wrap up your business?"

"I'll have to check my appointment book, but I'm sure I can fit you in there

somewhere." He capped.

Victoria grabbed the bulge in his pants, causing him to go up an octave. She brought her face an inch away from his and her Chanel #5 perfume invaded his nostrils. Staring into his eyes, she smiled harder and said, "Nobody likes a smart ass."

"Apparently you do." Still smiling, he tilted his head from left to right.

At that moment, Lafayette's cellular rang with a text message. He looked at it and it was Gar saying that he was ready.

"The boys must have finished loading up everything." Victoria assumed.

"Yep." He shot him a text back letting him know that he was on his way. Afterwards, he kissed the queen pin and bid her a farewell, heading for the door.

Chapter Five

That night

Batice played the corner of 84th and Figueroa smoking a square and holding tight to the strap of her purse. She was wearing a form fitting black dress that just made it to cover up her ass and high heel pumps. She smacked on gum and impatiently tapped her foot, while keeping her arms folded across her chest. About fifteen feet away, and hiding within the shadows was Theo, pretending to be on his cell phone. This was just a cover up though. He was really there watching out for Batice while she tried to pick up Johns. He used this strategy to throw the police off should they show up and start asking questions. Stashed in the front of his jeans was a .38 special with tape around its handle and trigger. Should drama arrive, he didn't have any plans to shoot it, he counted on selling Wolf Tickets and waving it around to thwart off any trouble. This was how much of a bitch ass nigga that he was.

Theo came up with the bright idea of having Batice sell her pussy out on the streets. After being deprived from crack for so long, little momma was down with whatever was going to score her some drugs. She didn't have any qualms with turning tricks. After being ran through by Loon and his camp she felt that there was nothing to it. Hell, she kind of liked it. Sex was the only thing she was particularly good at. It was a skill, and she was looking forward to parlaying it into money for her habit.

A Toyota pulled up on the block. Inside there was a Mexican man with a protruding gut. He leaned forth and smiled at Batice boasting his missing teeth. The teeth that were there were rotten and decaying. The Mexican man took a swallow from his Corona bottle and motioned her over. Batice was repulsed by the man. She blew hard and prepared to put on her best performance. She stepped forth and stuck her head inside of the window, smiling and chewing gum.

"How are you doing tonight, baby?" she asked the Mexican man.

"Me fine, baybe, how about ju?" he replied.

"I'm great, boo," She replied. "It's $60 for head and $200 for pussy. How do you want it, lover?" she licked her top lip seductively.

"Me want dee full ride, mama cita." He smiled and held up a wad of wrinkled bills.

"Well, you've just bought yourself a date, handsome." She snatched the door open and hopped into the passenger seat. "Pull around the corner here, sweetie."

A rental car came to a screeching halt beside the Mexican man's Toyota. The passenger stuck his .45 out of the window and into the driver's face. The passenger barked a threat and the Mexican man's eyes lit up with fear. He raised his hands up in surrender, dropping his bottle of beer on the floor of his vehicle and spilling its contents.

***

"So what were you and old girl talking about?" Gar asked from the passenger seat. He was slumped in the seat and looking out of the window. The sidewalk and its businesses showed on the front passenger side window's glass.

"Garza and his sister; she's going to take care of that situation for me."

"For real?" Gar asked. The hustler nodded. "You gotta love an old bitch with power."

"Yeah, looks like I hit the jackpot fucking with this old broad."

"How's the pussy?"

"Oh, it's fire, believe that." He replied, smiling. "Some of the best I done had."

"Be careful with that bitch, bruh. Them old bitches get a hold of young niggaz and try to run'em. They think niggaz like us are their toys and shit." Gar dropped game on him. "You ever see a selfish kid with his toys? The lil mothafucka doesn't want anybody else playing with his toys…even when he ain't playing with'em. The first thing he hollers is mine when he sees another kid with his shit."

"I'll keep that in mind. But right now I need this bitch in pocket. She's hitting us off with these squares and she's about to go to bat for us. I'd be a fool to back up off her now. I'm tryna ride this situation until the wheels fall off, feel me?"

Gar nodded his understanding. His eyes drifted back to the window. He saw something that caught his eye and made him sit up in his seat. "I know that ain't Batice?"

"Where?" A frowning Lafayette looked in the same direction.

"Right here," Gar pointed, face transforming into a scowl. "That is her, blood! Bust a bitch and pull up on this Toyota!" he unbuckled his safety belt and both of his .45s seemed to appear in his hands.

Lafayette brought a walkie-talkie to his lips. He held down a button and said, "Y'all continue to the rally point, man, but don't unload shit until we get there." He told the handlers that were driving the U-haul van. They were tailing them to make sure the birds reached their destination.

Gar let down the passenger side window. As soon as the car came to a screeching halt he stuck his .45 out of the window and into the driver of the Toyota's face. "Don't move,

60

mothafucka! Or I'll put cha face on that dashboard!" he barked. The Mexican man trembled with fear as he hands shot up in the air quivering. He didn't dare make a move, for fear that Gar would make good on his threat. "La, get Batice and put her in the car!" he ordered his Main Man.

Lafayette hopped out of the rental and stepped upon the curb, clutching his .9mm. He snatched open the passenger side door and pulled a terrified Batice out by her arm. He then put her in the backseat of his rental and stood outside of the door, holding his banger to his side, out of sight. He looked to the Mexican man inside of the Toyota. "Gone and get outta here, Amigo." The Mexican man drove off and Lafayette looked around to make sure there wasn't any police present.

Theo made to run but when Gar pointed both of his bangers in his direction he froze up. Trembling, he raised his hands into the air as his knees buckled. "You wanna run? Go ahead, I'll soak up that dingy ass hoodie!" he swore as he approached, scowling.

"What chu talking about, man? I'm not going anywhere!" Theo said.

Gar tucked one of his bangers into the front of his jeans and kept one trained on Theo. He grabbed him by the collar of his hoodie and forced him up against the liquor store. He pressed his steel into the side of his face, while mad dogging him. Theo's eyes were at their corners, hoping that the gun didn't go off and leave his brains on his right shoulder. He looked scared as a bitch.

"Didn't I tell you about fucking with my baby momma?" Gar asked. Theo didn't say a word. Instead, he closed his eyes tight and silently prayed to God. His bowels shifted and he felt like he was going to shit on himself. "I suggest you answer my question before this foe-fever gives you a lobotomy." Theo nodded yes, rapidly. "That's right, I did tell you, but chu didn't listen, yo bad." Gar stepped back, but kept his banger in that bitch ass nigga'z face. He kicked him in the balls and he made an "Oof" sound, grabbing his junk. His eyes watered and he dropped to his knees. Gar then grabbed him by the collar of his hoodie before he could hit the sidewalk. Afterwards, he took his banger by its barrel and cracked him across the head with it, repeatedly. Seeing that Theo's face was bloody and his eyes were rolled to their whites, Gar shoved his crimson stained banger into his mouth, all of the way down to its trigger-guard.

"You fucked up, nigga! Now that's yo ass!" Gar closed his eyes so blood wouldn't get in them, brushing his finger against the trigger. That's when he heard a noise at his rear. He looked over his shoulder and saw three little kids headed his way on bicycles. "Youz about a lucky, bitch!" he let Theo's body hit the sidewalk hard. He then tucked his .45 and hopped into the backseat of the rental beside Batice. "We're out this mothafucka!" he hollered up front to Lafayette and the rental sped away from the scene.

For a good twenty minutes Lafayette had rode the freeway listening to Gar hurl threats and insults at Batice. He sighed with relief once he finally arrived at their apartment.

"Take Lil Gar in the house, I'll be in there in a minute." Gar told Batice, hostility written across his face.

"Nah, it's cool, Gar, go ahead and take it in. You've had a long day." Lafayette told his homeboy.

"What chu mean, blood? We've got business that needs to be handled."

"I know that, and I'm on it. I'll make sure them thangs get where they need to be."

Gar blew hard and looked from his baby momma and son to his Main Man.

"All right, but if you need me bang my line." He stated seriously.

"I got chu faded." Gar touched fists with Lafayette and slid out of the rental, slamming the door shut behind him.

After dropping off Gar and Batice, Lafayette slid to the trap and made sure the birds got dropped off. He then made sure the other half got dropped off at his other spot. With that out of the way, Lafayette decided to drop by and see one of his ladies.

Chapter Six

Lafayette's love muscle was buried deep inside of her pussy as she sat atop of him. Her head was tilted back and her eyes were narrowed into slits. Her French manicured nails sunk into his chest as she rotated her hips in a circular motion. Her chest heaved up and down like a cheetah that chased down its prey. The sounds that escaped from her lips seemed inhuman. The bedroom was filled with both of their moans and groans. She grinded into him harder and faster, as he gripped her hips tightly. Lafayette held onto her so tight that his hands sunk into the soft flesh of her buttocks, the meat their seeping between his fingers. She sunk her nails deeper into his chest as she neared her orgasm. He bit down on his bottom lip, fighting the pain she caused when she tore into his hide. The burns he felt from the scratches to his chest were nothing compared to the euphoria she brought him to. She felt too good, there was no way he was going to stop her.

***

Jason came through the door toting his briefcase and loosening the tie around his neck. The day had been long and hard at the office and he couldn't wait to get home. The whole time he had his mind on the ice cold bottles of Miller's Genuine Draft in his refrigerator. His plan was to kick back, relax and watch the game in peace while he enjoyed a cold brew.

Jason sat his briefcase on the floor next to the coat-stand and hung up his overcoat. He headed into the kitchen and grabbed a cold one out of the refrigerator. He walked into the living room and picked up the remote control. He was about to turn on the "50 inch Samsung flat-screen, when he heard a woman moaning. He sat the bottle of beer down on the coffee-table along with the remote control. He headed up the steps and made his way down the hall. The closer he neared the master bedroom the louder the moans grew. In fact, the moans were no longer moans; they conformed to screams of passion.

Jason's froze in the middle of the hall. His heart dropped into the pit of his stomach and he started hyperventilating. Feeling like he was about to faint, he placed his hands on the walls on each side of him. He reached into his pocket and pulled out his asthma pump, shaking it up. He closed his eyes and calmed himself down before taking two quick puffs. Once his breathing was normal, he hurried down the staircase and darted into the kitchen. He snatched a Butcher's knife from out of the knife block and shot up the staircase, three steps at a time. His eyes were red and glassy. His jaws were clenched and boasted his coffee stained teeth. There were homicides on his mind: two of them.

"Oh, my God, Lafayette, I'ma 'bout to cum!" he heard his wife scream.

Jason stopped before his bedroom door and kicked it with all of his might. The door flew open sending a spray of splinters. Montrice recoiled against the headboard, wearing an expression of shock and embarrassment. She was wearing nothing but a bra and a black silk robe. Jason checked the closet, under the bed, and the bathroom that was conjoined to their bedroom. Finding nothing, he stopped in the bathroom doorway, scanning the bedroom for any traces of another man. There wasn't any. His eyes stopped on Montrice and the sleek metal vibrator she clutched in her hand. Realizing that he'd made an ass out of himself, Jason sat down on the bed and placed the Butcher's knife down on the nightstand. He brought his hands down his face and blew hard, looking back up. He then leaned forward with his elbows on his legs, clasping his hands together. Montrice crawled over to him and wrapped her arms around him. She placed gentle kisses on the side of his face and hugged him tightly.

"There's no one here but me, you're all I ever wanted in a man, Jason." She told him.

"Seriously?" he looked to her and asked.

"Yes." She kissed his lips tenderly.

"I'm sorry, it's just...I don't know." He looked away, shaking his head.

"Shhhh, it's OK, don't worry about it," she hugged him even tighter.

***

"Jesus," Victoria called out after catching her nut. She looked down at Lafayette with an amazing smile and captivating beauty. She leaned forth and kissed him passionately before falling on the side of him on the King size bed. She grabbed her gold case and her Zippo-lighter from off of the nightstand. She removed a neatly rolled joint from the case and slipped it between her full lips, putting fire to the end of it. With a flick of her wrist, she snapped the Zippo-lighter closed and tossed it back on the nightstand. Victoria took a few pulls from the joint and expelled white smoke. She then looked to Lafayette and said, "I need some fresh air," before stepping out onto the balcony of her bedroom, as naked as the day she was pulled out of her mother's womb.

Lafayette slipped on his boxer-briefs and joined the queen pin outside on the balcony.

"What's on your mind, Lafayette?" Victoria asked without looking at him. She was staring straight ahead and smoking her joint.

"Nothing," He lied. "I'm one hundred."

"Nah, something is eating you," She called his bluff, rubbing the side of his face.

"How you figure?"

"Your performance in bed was subpar, no offense." She told him. "You normally come with that thunder, but this time I could tell that you weren't really into it." she tilted her head back and blew out a cloud of white smoke. "Let me guess, it's about your little friend that's in County?"

He sighed and nodded. "Yeah, I don't know how I'm going to play this. My livelihood is on the line."

"You want my advice?" she finally looked to him.

"You have been doing your thang for a time now; your input to me is invaluable."

"Don't allow your feelings for this guy to taint your judgment. Your emotions are your enemies in situations like these. It's always better to use your head. Fuck feelings."

"Are you saying that I should have'em whacked out?" lines creased his forehead.

"I'm saying you should make the best decision for you and your business." She corrected him. "Trust your instincts. I always do. It's the reason that I've prospered in this business for the past twenty-eight years." She flicked what was left of her joint away. "Come on. Let's go back to bed; you can make up for that lackluster performance earlier." She grasped his hand and led him back inside of the bedroom.

***

Savon was lying on his bunk flipping through the pages of a XXL magazine. When his eyes came across the Eye Candy section there was a shapely, butterscotch complexion vixen on the sleek page. Savon whistled as he feasted his eyes on video model's bodacious body.

He couldn't help but imagine himself bending her over a pool table and having his way with her. Back on the outside he had enough paper and juice to make that thought come true. The problem was he wasn't on the outside he was locked up. The closes thing to pussy he was going to get to was his fist.

Savon slicked his right palm with Vaseline. He was just about to dip it into his pants when he felt his cell phone vibrating under his pillow. He wiped his hand on the mattress and pulled a bulky sock from underneath his pillow. He peeled back four layers of socks before he reached his mini flip phone. He flipped it open, pressed "answer" and placed it to his ear.

"What's up, Gar?" he spoke into the flip phone. "I'm two-hundred, loved one. Yeah, I know exactly who that is. I can make it happen, but it's gone run you a lil something. Smooth. Well, let me make a couple of calls and see what I can put together. All right," He ended the call and placed another one. "What's up, Y.G?"

"Savon, what that shit do, blood?" the voice spoke from the other end of the phone.

"I need a favor."

"Speak on it, big homie."

Chapter Seven

Lil Man stood on the top tier eating an orange while resting his arms on the guardrail. He looked down on the floor at the inmates that had amassed. They were either playing cards, shooting the shit or talking on the telephone. The convicts' mesh of voices sounded identical to the ones inside of a middle school cafeteria.

Lil Man was doing a little more than playing the tier and eating his orange. He was also acting as lookout for the cell behind him. At the moment one of his whores was inside servicing a John. Pimping was a trade that Lil Man picked up when he hit the County. It afforded him the finer things behind the walls and kept his mind off of his ordeal.

Every down-low inmate was coming to holler at Lil Man for some jail house pussy. They loved fucking with his whores. Though his bitches were men most of them had big silicone breasts and hips thanks to Botox injections. Hell, some of them even had the sex operation done and boasted artificial vaginas. The fellas ate that up. It wasn't the real thing, but it was close enough to them.

"Uh…yeah, that a girl!" a man's shaky voice came from the cell. Anyone listening could tell he was being sexually pleasured.

The blanket that was hanging on the string that stretched across the cell was pulled back, and a potbelly white man with a thick grayish mustache emerged. He pulled the blanket back and came out of the cell, zipping up his jump suit. He gave Lil Man a nod and went on about his business.

"Another satisfied customer," Lil Man smiled to himself.

Another inmate approached Lil Man just as the potbelly white man was leaving. He was a tall, skinny dude with a peanut shape head and a dagger tattooed between his eyes. His knuckles bore old cuts and gashes from fights, many of them that were fought out on the street. He tapped Lil Man on the shoulder and he turned around to him. They chopped it up for a second before the little nigga ducked off into the cell. When he entered his whore, Ruby, was standing over the metal sink spitting jizz into the bowl, watching roll down inside of the drain. Once she'd finished, she gargled with Listerine and spat it back out.

"Ruby, I gotta trick out here that wants the works." Lil Man told her, one side of his jaw full of food. "You up for it? Or do you wanna take your break right now?"

74

Ruby pulled her dark burgundy hair back into a ponytail and looked herself over in the mirror, taking in her reflection.

"Send him in, suga." She said in a feminine, southern voice, a hint of masculinity in it.

"Cool." Lil Man took a bite out of his orange. When he turned to leave peanut head closed the door on him. "Mothafucka, open this door." He pounded on the door with his fist. "Open up this door or when I get outta here, I'ma beat cho ass!" he hollered at the rectangle shaped window where he could see peanut head's smiling face.

Lil Man went to turn around and Rudy grabbed him from behind, wrapping her arm around his neck as tightly as she could. She then produced a 7 inch metal shank from the small of her back and stabbed him in his back six times, rapidly. She released Lil Man's neck and let him fall to the floor. Rudy stood there watching him gasp for air as he held his bleeding back. She kissed her fingers tips and touched them to his cheek, The Black Hand of Death. She then dropped the shank into the toilet bowl and flushed it down.

Lil Man lay on his side clutching his back as his blood coated the floor. His vision became blurry, while his breathing became sporadic and loud. His eyes blinked a couple of times and his breathing slowed, before he knew it darkness claimed him.

***

Lafayette pulled up to the train station and parked in the red zone. He hopped out of his rental and stepped upon the curb. He pulled out his cell phone and glanced at the time as he walked towards the entrance. It wasn't that he was looking to catch a train; this particular station had one of the only in service phone booths and he was expecting a very important phone call. Seeing what time it was, Lafayette put some pep into his step. Nearing the phone booth, he saw that someone was already there.

Lafayette stepped to the dude that was already on the telephone. He was a stocky dude rocking a goatee and a black snap-back with a yellow P on the front. Lafayette waited a few seconds before tapping him on the shoulder. The stocky dude turned around wearing a hard-face, looking like he was about ready to snap.

"I need that line freed, homie, I'm waiting for an important call." Lafayette told him.

"And? Fuck outta here!" the stocky dude scowled and waved him off.

Lafayette sighed and massaged the bridge of his nose. He then tapped the stocky dude on his shoulder again.

"Hold on, Baby, I'ma 'bout to whip this nigga'z ass." The stocky dude spoke into the telephone. He dropped the phone and it snagged on its cord. He turned his snapback backwards and tucked his gold Rolex chain. He turned around to Lafayette ready to loosen his front teeth. The hustler pulled his jacket aside so that the stocky dude could see the handle of his banger, which was on his hip. The stocky dude raised his hands in surrender. He was wearing a terrified expression. Lafayette threw his head towards the door and the stocky dude stepped off.

He picked up the telephone and hung it up. Afterwards, he rested his arm on top of the phone booth and patiently waited for his important call. A minute later the telephone rang; he snatched it up and placed it to his ear. He didn't utter a word, he just listened. For a time the line was silent and then a voice said "It's done".

The person on the other side of the telephone hung up while Lafayette stood there holding the phone to his ear. He took the time to gather himself before hanging up the telephone and starting for the exit.

Lil Man was gone and so was the possibility of him ever snitching. And though Lafayette should have been relieved about this, he most certainly wasn't. He felt like the biggest piece of shit in the world. He had just had a friend of his murdered all because he wasn't for sure if he was going to rat or not. No matter what way he tried to look at it he'd never be able to be alright with himself. For as long as he lived, Lil Man's death would weigh on his soul.

***

Montrice was down on her knees, gripping the sides of the commode and throwing up. Once she was done she sat on the filthy restroom floor and sat up against the graffiti sprawled stall's wall. She looked down at her black police uniform and saw a stain by the collar she'd gotten from her vomiting. She rolled her hand in a length of toilet paper and tore it free. After rubbing out as much of the stain as she could, she folded the toilet paper and wiped her mouth. She then threw the soiled toilet paper into the commode and flushed it down. She bent her knees to her chest and wrapped her arms around them, bowing her head between them.

Montrice had been throwing up for the past couple of days. At first, she thought it was from the spicy Indian food that she ate, but then she started to believe that she was pregnant. Especially after speaking with her mother and discovering she had a dream about fishes. She checked the calendar for the date that she and Lafayette had unprotected sex. The date matched up with the date she began throwing up. And on top of all of that, she'd missed her period. If she truly was pregnant she didn't know how she was going to break it to Jason. There wasn't any telling how he was going to react. She'd witnessed how he reacted when he thought she was having sex with another man so she could only imagine what kind of shit storm it would bring when she broke the news of her pregnancy by another man. Then she thought about Lafayette. How would he take to her being knocked up with his seed? Would he embrace her with love and open arms, or shun her and cast her away. She didn't know how things would play out and it wasn't any use of her thinking up different scenarios because she didn't know for sure if she was pregnant for sure.

Montrice took a few minutes to pull herself together. She then got to her feet and shuffled out of the stall. She took a good look at herself in the cracked, dirt smudged mirror and turned on the faucet. She cupped her hands under the flowing water and splashed the water onto her face. She took a deep breath, and tore a few paper towels free. She dabbed her face dry, balled the paper towels up and threw it into the trash can as she headed out.

When Montrice came out of the restroom, she found her diesel partner leant up against the back of the police cruiser with his massive biceps folded across his chest. He was a six foot one white dude and he rocked a shaved head. His eyes were hidden by black sunglasses and he was chewing gum. A smile was stretched across his face.

"Are you all right there, partner?" he asked.

"I'll be OK. Just remind me not to eat the enchiladas from that joint again."

"I got cha. Are you ready to go?"

"Yeah, just let me grab a few things outta this gas station."

"Be a pal and grab me a Yoohoo, would ya?"

"Sure." Montrice made her way into the gas station's store. She had a couple of items on her mind to grab, but the one at the top of her list was a pregnancy test.

Chapter Eight

That night

"Shit, it's hot as hell in here, girl." Auntie said to Diana as she fanned herself with a folded news paper. They were hard at work inside of the tiny kitchen whipping Lafayette's powder into crack cocaine. The entire house was an inferno, even the walls were sweating. They had an 18 inch fan in the corner circulating air, but it was little help against the sweltering heat.

"Boo, you ain't never lied." Diana wiped the sweat that dripped from her brow with the back of her latex gloved hand. She took a pull from her cigarette and went back to the task of whipping the cocaine up inside of the clear Pyrex pot.

The two workers, who were hard at work at the kitchen table, were catching it too. One had his shirt off while the other's wife-beater was drenched. Their bodies were wet and glistening. It looked like they'd rubbed baby oil all over their bodies. They were busy chopping rocks and bagging them up.

"I'm 'bout to die in this mothafucka, on God." This was the worker wearing the drenched wife-beater. He wiped his face with the palm of his hand and went back to cutting the crack with a Gemstar razor.

"Fuck, man, it's a real live sweat shop out this bitch." The bare chest worker voiced his opinion. His skinny body was plastered with tattoos. He looked more like a tattoo artist than a D-boy. "Shit!" he snatched his bottle of water from the table and poured it all over his face. He smacked it back down on the table and went back to the task assigned to him.

"Fuck this!" Wife-beater shot to his feet and snatched his joint off the table. He tucked it into the front of his Levi's.

"Where you going, foolie?" The skinny tattooed dude asked.

"I'm 'bout to run up to Rite Aid and cop an A/C." Wife-beater picked up his jacket from the back of his chair.

"Oh, thank God." Diana said, looking like a runaway slave.

"Thank you, baby," Auntie told him.

Wife-beater nodded and made a beeline towards the front-door. He unchained and unlocked the door, snatching it open. As soon as wife-beater's foot stepped across the threshold, he was walking back inside, .357 Magnum revolver inside of his grill. Wife-beater had his hands held high in the air as Zay forced him back into the house, with La'Chat by his side.

"Oh, fuck!" The skinny tattooed dude shot to his feet and reached for his burner on the table. His fingers had just curled around the handle of his thang when a slugs slammed into his stomach and his chest. He grimaced and staggered back, bumping into the wall and sliding down to the floor, leaving a crimson smear.

"Anybody else wanna see who's the fastest gun in the East?" La'Chat barked from behind a stocking, turning her smoking Desert Eagle on Auntie and Diana. The older women had their hands in the air and shook their heads slowly no. "Y'all bring your asses in here and lay on your stomachs." The women did as they were told.

"I'ma take this here revolver outta your pie-hole." Zay told Wife-beater. He was wearing a stocking over his face too. "Don't try no slick shit, ya hear?" Wife-beater nodded. The mountain of muscle slowly pulled his .357 Magnum revolver out of wife-beater's mouth, bringing along a length of saliva that lead from his mouth to the end of his weapon's barrel. He then pulled the banger from wife-beater's waist and shoved it into his coat's pocket. "Take this duct-tape and bound them old bitches mouths, wrists and ankles over there." He handed wife-beater the duct-tape that he'd taken from within the confines of his coat.

"Shit, man, I need a medic 'fore I bleed to death." The skinny tattooed dude touched his stomach and came away with a bloody palm. He was bleeding out of his mouth too.

"You should have thought about that before you tried to draw iron, bitch boy." La'Chat told him as she stood over him with her Desert Eagle pointed at the top of his dome.

Once wife-beater finished bounding Auntie and Diana with duct-tape, he stood off to the side with his hands up.

"All right y'all, I see you got the cocaine up in this piece, but where them grips at?" Zay asked, looking around at all of the niggaz that occupied the living room. No one said a word. They were all terrified. "Somebody better tell me something before I start nodding heads in here." He gave them all his threatening eyes.

"There's ain't no money in here, dawg." Wife-beater spoke up. "All they keep in here is the product."

"Why you lying to me, man?" Zay asked.

"I'm not lying to you, bruh. That's real shit." Wife-beater assured. "Dude come by here every few hours and pick his up."

"Lay on your stomach with your hands on your head."

"Ah, come on, man, you gone peel me for keeping it one hunnit?" he looked at him like he couldn't believe that he would do such a thing.

"Nigga, don't make me tell you again!" Zay's nose scrunched up. Once wife-beater did as he was told, the muscle bound bandit marched over to the skinny tattooed dude and pulled him to his feet, causing him to yelp. He clutched him at the back of his neck and slammed him face down into a mountain of cocaine, holding him there. The skinny nigga tried to resist, but his wounds left him too weak to put up a decent fight. His arms flailed wildly sending clouds of white powder into the air.

Zay stared wife-beater dead in his eyes as he suffocated the skinny tattooed dude, body slightly rocking from left to right due to his victim's fighting for his life. Zay wore a face deprived of sympathy or remorse. Killing was as easy as reciting the letters of The Alphabet to him. The skinny tattooed dude's flailing arms grew slower and slower until they finally stopped, dropping off to the sides of him. Zay released the back of the skinny tattooed dude's neck and he fell back on the floor, his face coated with powder and his eyes staring out of their corners.

"You wanna tell me where that paper is now, big dawg?" Zay asked wife-beater. His eyes were red and glassy. Tears had welled up in his eyes and spilled down his cheeks, pelting the carpet. He nodded yes. "I thought you would."

Once wife-beater told them where the money was stashed and La' Chat headed off into the bedroom. "Bingo!" she called out from the bedroom once she recovered the loot, stretching a smile across Zay's face.

Zay looked to wife-beater and pointed his .357 Magnum revolver at his dome. "It's hammer time!" he said, pulling the trigger.

BOOM!

***

"Yo they hit the trap." Lafayette old Gar. "Niggaz took forty bands and six birds."

"Who?" Gar frowned.

"I don't know, but there were two of them. A big dude and a girl; I'm leaning towards Zay and La'Chat."

"Is everybody OK?"

"Mooty and Kay Kay bought it. They left Auntie and Diana alive, though."

"Man, them two strung out bitches probably were in on the whole shit."

"I don't think so. They were way fucked up behind how it went down."

"I know better." Gar assured him, "Nothing comes between a head and their fix. Them bitches know something and I'ma get it out of'em." He snatched his black Bomber jacket

86

with the fur around the hood from out of the closet and stashed his .45s into the front of his Levi's. "Come on." He told Lafayette as he headed for the door, slapping his black White Sox snapback with the gray brim on his dome.

"Where are you going, Gar?" Batice asked from where she sat on the couch. She had Little Gar in her arms. He was giggling and flailing his arms around, watching Sponge Bob.

Lafayette took in Batice's appearance. She looked very sickly. Her eyes had bags under them and black rings. Her face was dry and ashy. She looked nauseated. He'd seen this look before in crackheads. She was jonesing for a fix. Her habit was wreaking havoc on her.

"Finna bust this move with La. What's up?"

"Can you stop by the store and get me some pads, please?"

"I got chu." Gar kissed Batice and then his son goodbye.

"Baby momma looks sick, fam. You should probably take her to the 'spital or something." Lafayette said as they walked down the steps.

"Yeah, I'ma take her to rehab in the A.M. I found this place out in Orange County." Gar told him. "I looked it up on the web. It's a real clean lil spot. It's a few bands a month but I can afford it."

***

Batice carried Little Gar over to the window and peeked between the blinds. She watched as Lafayette and her baby daddy drove off in his rental. She then bopped off to the bedroom, where she pulled open the closet door and took down a shoe box. She sat the shoe box on the bed and flipped off the lid. Next, she pulled out the red Hush Puppy and reached inside of it. She removed a bulging black dress sock and emptied its contents out on the bed: twelve bankrolls held together by rubber-bands.

"What's that, June June? Can you say money?" She kissed Little Gar's chubby cheek. She removed the rubber-band from around the bankroll and pulled six Big Face Benjamin's free. She then rolled the bills back up; slipped the rubber-band back over them and stuffed them back into the black dress sock along with the other bankrolls.

Batice folded up the money and stuffed it into her bra. She placed the shoe box back into the closet where she found it and snatched up the keys to Gar's Magnum. She slipped on her famous liquor store shades and bopped towards the door. She was on her way to making some hustler a few hundred dollars richer.

Chapter Nine

"Goddamn, Theo, what the fuck happened to you?" Loon asked as he examined his cousin's face. Gar had done quite a number on him. His eye was swollen shut, his nose was broken and the side of his face was twice its size.

"Niggaz jumped me and took my scratch." Theo lied. "Caught me slipping when I came outta the liquor store."

"Nigga, if you don't knock it off!" Loon waved him off, not believing his story. "You ran into dude that caught chu with that skeeza again, didn't chu? He put the beats on yo ass again, didn't he?" Theo hung his head and nodded yes. Loon shook his head and fired up the blunt he prepared before his cousin came knocking on his door. "I knew it, you didn't even have to say so. You gotta do something about this, Theo, or its gone keep happening. At least as long as you keep fucking with that broad it is. And you don't have any intentions on quitting that bitch, do you?" Theo looked up into his cousin's eyes and shook his head no. "That's what I figured. You can't let this shit slide. You gone have to let'em know that cho heart don't pump no Kool-Aid."

"I know, cousin, I'ma handle mine." Theo sat down on the couch.

"No you not." Loon called his bluff. "You're gonna get White Boy wasted and rant and rave about how you're gonna rock this dude to sleep until you pass out drunk, like you always do, you lousy mothafucka."

"How you know, cuz?" Theo asked, taking the blunt from Loon.

"'Cause I know you, nigga, I can't let chu let this one go. You're gonna have me looking bad out here. How's it gonna look when cats see my peoples walking around the hood looking like Mayweather's sparring partner? That's the kind of shit that'll tarnish my rep out here in these streets. Dudes may think I went soft and try me for something. You know I'm doing my thang out here." Loon was laying it on thick. The cats around his way knew his crew and how they loved to play with guns so they gave them a wide berth. The truth of the matter was that nigga just lived for the drama. It made his dick hard. Theo's situation gave him the perfect excuse to bring his toys out.

Theo blew out a cloud of white smoke and thought on it for a moment. "All right, when are you tryna do this?"

"Shit, right now." Loon rose to his feet and disappeared inside of his bedroom. He returned with an AK-47 with a banana clip the shape of a capital Jay. He smiled like a kid who'd received the toy that he'd wanted for Christmas. "You ready to lay a fuck-nigga down?" Theo nodded and took the choppa from his cousin's hands. He tested its weight and aimed it at something across the living room. "Yeaaah, that's what I'm talking about, it's time to get active with this nigga." Loon smiled wickedly and rubbed his hands together.

***

They hung from the steel pipe in the basement. Their wrists bonded by handcuffs and their mouths stuffed with red ball gags. Their bodies were wet and dripping on the floor, droplets splashing on the surface. Their backs were red and throbbing with thick welts. One of their eyes was rolled to their whites. This person was barely conscious and had thrown up through the gag ball. The other person was still up and very alert. They were being punished not for something that they necessarily did, but for something they may have done. The verdict was still up in the air, seeing how neither of them had yet to breakdown and confess their involvement in said violation.

The thick black leather belt whistled through the air as it was uncoiled by its wielder.

SWHACK!

SWHACK!

SWHACK!

The belt caused its target to jump with each strike it landed on its hide. The target went stiff and then hung limply from the steel pipe. They'd had enough. Their body couldn't take it any longer. It had taken all that it could stand before giving in.

"You hoes ain't getting outta this until you tell me who these niggaz are and where they at with our shit." Gar wrapped the thick leather belt around both of his fists, coiling and uncoiling it. "If I gotta beat chu bitches to death I will, either way somebody's gone pay." He looked to Lafayette who was looking at Diana and Auntie with pity. Something in his head told him to let the women go, but something else told him *"fuck them bitches, they helped them mothafuckaz run off with your shit."* Lafayette was feeling conflicted. He didn't really know how he wanted to play this situation. What he did know is that he was going to get his shit back, one way or another.

"Nigga, did you hear me?" Gar frowned.

Lafayette snapped back to the now. "Huh? Oh, what's cracking?"

"Hose this bitch down." He pointed his belt at Auntie. "Somebody gone talk."

Hearing that, Lafayette's face transformed into a mask of hatred. He pointed the water hose gun at Auntie's back and pulled the trigger, soaking her back up. While he was doing this, Gar was slipping off his white T-shirt. He tossed it aside and donned his wife-beater. He gave Lafayette the signal to stop and he cocked the hand wielding the belt back. He whipped Auntie's back until the skin split and bled. When he finished he was breathing hard. His chest was heaving up and down, rapidly. Madness was bleeding from his eyes. He looked like he had gone insane.

Gar hung the belt around his neck and stepped to the old rusty metal table against the wall. He snatched up the big bucket of salt water and approached Auntie. He splashed her back with the salt water and she danced around on the steel pipe. When the salt water hit Auntie's open wounds it felt like someone had set her back on fire. She attempted to scream but the gag ball muffled her cries.

Gar sat the bucket of salt water down by his leg and snatched the belt from around his neck. He stepped behind Diana, coiling and uncoiling his black leather belt.

He looked to Lafayette. "Soak this bitch up, La."

Lafayette nodded and proceeded to wet Diana up with the water hose gun.

***

"I...I don't think I can go through with this, Loon." Theo stammered nervously. "I don't know if I'm built for a body."

"You're right, shit don't feel right." Loon agreed, nodded his head. "You wanna just take it back home?"

Theo nodded. "Yeah, man, let's just go back to the house."

Loon smacked that hoe ass nigga upside the head. "Do you hear yourself? I'm ashamed to call you my fucking cousin. Do you know what you sound like right now? A Chrome cold bitch! That's what chu sound like, man! Grow a pair and let'em hang!" He shook his head and massaged the bridge of his nose. "You know what? Fuck that! This nigga gone like yesterday! You ain't gotta pop the mothafucka, I'll handle 'em." He pulled the Nike baseball gloves down over each of his hands tightly and flexed his fingers. He pulled the black bandana up over the lower half of his face. He checked the banana clip of his AK-47, placed it back into the slot and smacked it in.

Theo wanted to protest further but decided to keep his mouth shut. He didn't want Loon to get pissed off and beat his ass. He'd once seen him pistol whip a man to a bloody pulp over a five dollar bag of Sess. He never wanted to end up on the receiving end of that brutal assault. He'd rather go along with the flow and avoid a hospital stay.

"This is the street right here, ain't it?" Loon asked. Theo nodded and made the turn. "Maroon Magnum, Outlaws on the plates, that's him pulling off. Keep the lights on and creep slowly. I'll catch'em at the intersection."

***

Batice pulled away from the curb in front of her apartment building. She changed the channel on the stereo until she found something she wanted to listen to. Kendrick Lamar's *Poetic Justice* came ripping through the speakers. She turned the volume up loud, dancing and spitting the lyrics to it. She looked to Little Gar, who was strapped in the front seat inside of the baby seat and tickled his chin. He smiled and looked at her. Batice made a left at the corner en route to the intersection. She was oblivious to the Dodge Intrepid following her. She was too in tuned with the music to pay attention to anything else.

***

Loon let the window down and cocked the hammer on his assault rifle. He looked to Theo and said, "Roll up on this mothafucka, right next to the driver side window."

Theo was sweating like he'd just run a marathon. His heart was beating wildly inside of his chest. It felt as if it was trying to punch through his left-breast. He was scared as shit and didn't know how to tell Loon no. He wiped his sweaty palms off on his shirt and took a hold of the steering-wheel. He mashed the gas pedal and sped towards the Magnum. Loon gripped his assault rifle with both hands and licked his chops. A wicked smile stretched across his face. The anticipation of catching a body gave him a rush like no other. It was like a shot of adrenaline.

***

Fire ripped through Diana's back as the black leather belt pierced her hide. She tried screaming but the gag ball in her mouth didn't allow much sound to escape. Her face was coated with perspiration and tears. Gar pulled back and was about to let the black leather belt have ago at her again, when Lafayette raised a hand and stopped him.

"What's popping, blood?" Gar asked. He was bare chest and his body was glistening from sweat. His chest bulged and fell as he breathed. He grabbed a bottle of water that was sitting by the steps and screwed off the top. He took the bottle to the head, finishing it off. He crushed the bottle of water with his hand and tossed it to the side. Whipping mothafuckas was hard work. It quenched his thirst.

"She's trying to say something." Lafayette told him.

"Now we're getting somewhere." Gar hung the black leather belt around his neck and walked around to Diana. He pulled the gag ball out of her mouth and listened to what she had to say.

"We…We didn't have anything to do with y'all trap getting robbed." Diana told him weakly, eyes hooded. "Those people broke in and took the money and the dope. They left us alive to tell the tale. I swear to God, I put that on my kids. You've gotta believe me." She sobbed loudly.

"Well, I don't…so I guess it's back to the drawing board." Gar put the gag ball back into her mouth. "Old head, I bet chu never had a hot hanger shoved up inside your pussy, huh?" he waited for her to answer, but when she didn't he continued, "I figured that. Well, it's a first time for everything."

"Nah, man, let'em loose." Lafayette told him.

"What?" Gar frowned.

"You heard what I said, nigga."

"La, I know you aren't falling for that bullshit ass story."

"I believe her."

Gar thought on it. "We can't just let'em go like that. They'll run and shoot their mouths off to One Time and have'em all up and through our shit."

Lafayette pulled the gag ball out of Auntie's mouth. She was barely conscience as she hung limp from the steel pipe. Her head was leant against her arm and her eyes were rolled to their whites.

"Auntie, if I let ya'll go are y'all gone run to them people?" Lafayette asked her seriously.

"No, I won't tell anyone, I promise." Diana spoke ahead of Auntie. "Y'all don't ever have to worry about me."

Lafayette turned his eyes from Diana, looking back to Auntie. "What's up, O.G? Let a nigga know something."

"No…" Auntie swallowed. "I'm not no snitch."

"Turn'em loose," Lafayette told Gar.

"This is some bullshit, man."

"I didn't ask you what it was."

Gar mumbled something under his breath and pulled the handcuff key from his pocket. He then moved to release the women from their handcuffs.

"It's hammer time…" Diana spoke.

"What did you say?" Lafayette asked, brushing past Gar.

"That's what the big dude said before he shot Kay Kay in the face."

While Gar was busy unlocking Auntie and Diana's handcuffs, Lafayette was thinking about what Diana had said. "It's hammer time," he'd heard that said to him by someone before, but he couldn't remember who it was. The catch phrase was so familiar. Something inside of his head clicked like the trigger of an empty gun. He snapped his fingers and said, "I know who hit us."

"Who?" Gar came over to him after releasing Auntie from her handcuffs.

***

Theo's car jerked to a stop beside the Magnum. Loon stuck his body half way out of the window and pulled the trigger. The choppa got off twice before a shell jammed it. Loon cursed it and ducked back inside. By the time he'd un-jammed the weapon, the Magnum was speeding through the intersection.

"Follow that mothafucka!" Loon barked at his cousin.

Theo floored the gas pedal and went after the Magnum.

***

"Shit, what the fuck was that?" Batice cursed. She was scared as hell and her body was trembling; Little Gar was screaming and crying inside of his baby seat. The firing of the choppa was loud and had startled him. Batice was slumped down in her seat. She stared into her rearview mirror as she drove recklessly, swooping in and out of lanes.

"Shhhh!" she hushed Little Gar. "It's OK, June June. Eve-rything is going to be all right, momma's baby." When Batice saw the Dodge Intrepid speeding up in the side-view mirror, her brain blared with an alarm "Danger! Danger! Danger!" "Oh, my God, this mothafucka is still on me!" she cried. Tears welled up in her eyes and spilled down her pale cheeks. Batice gripped the steering-wheel tight and floored the gas pedal, increasing the Magnum's speed. She dipped in and out of lanes, narrowly missing other cars on the street. She took the time to steal a glance from the side-view mirror to see where the Dodge Intrepid was. When she turned back around, a Metro Bus was making a wide turn before her. Batice pulled the steering-wheel to the right and slammed on the brakes. The Magnum swerved to the right and flipped over three times, coming apart.

***

"That mothafucka flipped three times, you know that nigga dead," Theo made the analysis after seeing the Magnum come apart once it flipped over so many times.

"For all we know God may have smiled upon his black ass." Loon spoke his mind as he eyed the wrecked Magnum. "Pull through so I can confirm this nigga'z death."

"Cousin, are you crazy?" Theo looked at him as if he had lost his mind. "You hear them sirens, The Boys are on their way."

Loon snarled and pointed the AK-47 in Theo's face. At the threat of the weapon his bitch ass cousin shut his mouth. His eyes bugged and fear gripped his heart. "Nigga, you gone either pull through there so I can see if this sucka is dead, or I'ma let this bitch off in your face! Make a choice!" he pressed his choppa into Theo's cheek.

"OK, all right." Theo nodded rapidly.

Theo and Loon stared inside of the ruined Magnum as they coasted by. Everything seemed to be moving in slow motion. Theo's eyes bugged and his mouth dropped open, when he saw a bloodied and barely conscious Batice. He peered closer when he saw the flailing arm of a baby and heard it cries.

"You stupid mothafucka," Loon punched Theo in the jaw. The Dodge Intrepid almost drifted into the next lane and collided into another car, but he grabbed control of the steering-wheel. "You had me thumping on that bitch and her fucking baby! Nigga, I should push your shit back!" he sneered at Theo and balled his fist so tight that they turned white at the knuckles. Theo cowered in his seat and shielded his face with his arm.

"I can't fucking believe you, man!" Loon punched the ceiling heatedly.

***

"That nigga Zay gotta relative from the hood, we call'em Mayo 'cause he a pale skinned nigga. He sort of looks like an Albino." Gar informed Lafayette. "We can pull his sleeve and try to get some info."

"You think he's gone tell us where his people holed up at?"

"Depends on how we go about asking 'em."

"Got cha."

"Ain't that Theo's punk ass?" Gar's face balled up and he pointed his finger at the windshield. He locked eyes with the nigga that turned his baby momma out, homie looked terrified.

"What the hell happened up here? That looks like your shit." Lafayette referred to the Magnum. He narrowed his eyes into slits and looked closer into the windshield.

"That is my shit!" Gar looked through the windshield. "Stop the car!" he unbuckled the safety belt. When the car stopped, he hopped out and ran over to the scene.

When he approached the wrecked Magnum he saw a bloodied Batice being strapped down on a gurney by paramedics. He kneeled down and looked in the ruined vehicle. His son wasn't in the baby seat. Worried, he grabbed one of the paramedic's by the arm and turned them around. "Where's my son? Fuck y'all do with my son?" he barked.

"Aye, homie," a voice came from Gar's rear. When he turned around a light skinned dude in a black tank top and camouflage shorts was holding his son. Little Gar's face was slick with tears. "This your lil dude?" Gar nodded. He thanked the light skinned dude and scooped up his son. He kissed his cheeks and asked him was he okay?

"Is your girl gonna be all right?" the light skinned dude inquired.

"Man, fuck that bitch!" Gar waved the mention of Batice off. "I got my lil man so I'm straight." He walked off towards Lafayette's rental.

Chapter Ten

Lafayette sat in the waiting room alongside Gar. He tossed back honey roasted peanuts while they talked.

"So you're sure it was that fool Theo you saw tonight?" Lafayette wanted to be sure.

"I'm positive." Gar answered. He was holding Little Gar in his arms. "I locked eyes with that mothafucka. It was him and some of other fuck-nigga. The driver side window of my car was blown out and there were two holes in the passenger side door. Them fools could have killed my son. The bullet went right above his head." he sat up in his seat, clenching his fists. "My whip got limo tints. They shot my shit up thinking I was inside. Whoever was riding with Theo was the trigger-man 'cause he ain't got the Chromes to bust a move like that. They fucked up though, 'cause now I'm on their ass."

Lafayette sat up and turned to face his Main Man. "You know where this fool laying his head?"

Gar shook his head. "Nah, but I can find out. And when I do, I'ma extinguish both of their lives, feel me?"

"If you getting down, you know I got chu."

"You ain't gotta do shit but watch me work."

"I hear you. I'm just letting you know, whatever you're up against your Day-One got cho back." He dapped him up.

"All day," Gar replied.

"You can see her now." The heavy set nurse told Gar.

"Hold your nephew until I come back." Gar passed Lafayette Little Gar and started for the door.

***

Gar stepped into the doorway of Batice's room. The room was dark, save for the light that illuminated the upper half of her from above. Gar approached her bedside. She was hooked up to a host of medical machinery. Her blonde braids were sprawled over her pillow exposing her entire face. Her face was littered with tiny cuts. Her brow was swollen and her arm and leg were in a cast. She was peacefully asleep.

Gar caressed the side of her face lovingly. "Baby, are you awake? It's Gar."

Batice's eyes fluttered open and she looked up at her baby daddy. He was smiling. "Girl, you scared the living shit outta me. I thought you and our son were dead. How are you feeling?"

Batice parted her lips and said, hoarsely, "Horrible."

"You'll be all right; we're gone get through this, all right?"

"All right," She slightly nodded.

"Baby, where were you going when you got into the accident?" she looked away and closed her eyes. "You were going to buy crack, weren't you?" tears shot down her cheeks hearing that. "It's OK, you can answer me. I know it isn't your fault, it's the drugs. They take over you. Believe me I know. I saw what that shit done to my daddy."

Batice looked to her first love. "Yes, I was going to buy crack. Oh, Gar, I'm so sorry." Tears welled up in her eyes and spilled down her cheeks. Little momma broke down sobbing hard, snot threatening to fall from her nose.

There was a click sound when Gar turned off the light illuminating the upper half of her. "It's OK, boo, I forgive you." He kissed her forehead gently. Slyly, while he performed this action, he turned off the heart monitor. Then suddenly, he clamped his hand down over her nose and mouth, smothering her. His face transformed into something demonic looking and he tightened his jaws, muscles pulsating in them. Batice tried to put up a fight but it was difficult to do with one arm. Gar placed his freehand over the one he was using to smother Batice with, adding more pressured and assuring oxygen wouldn't seep in between his fingers. He looked over both of his shoulders as he handled his business, making sure that no one was watching him or coming down the hall. He then turned his hateful eyes back on his baby momma. Saliva dripped from his lips as he fought her futile attempts to fight him off. The nigga put all of his weight onto his hands, forcing her deeper into the pillow. The swinging of Batice's arm grew weaker and slower the longer he smothered her. Before long her lone arm dropped and hung off the side of the bed. Gar wiped his palm off on her blanket. He then placed her arm beside her on the bed. Her turned the light above her on and left the room as quietly as he came.

Gar had enough of Batice. She'd fucked around on him, stole from him, got hooked on crack and had almost gotten their son killed. Yes, she had almost gotten their son killed. If it wasn't for her fooling around with Theo she would have never gotten hooked on crack and he would have never beaten his ass. Therefore, Theo wouldn't have been stalking the streets looking to kill him. The way he saw it, Batice had become a disease and he was the remedy.

Punk ass hoe, put my lil nigga'z life in danger, rest in shit, bitch. He disappeared through the doorway.

***

After dropping Little Gar off at his mother's house, Gar and Lafayette dipped back through the hood looking for Mayo. It was about two o'clock in the morning, so the streets were deathly quiet. Though the night was cool and calm, something was always on the rise in the ghetto, when the moon resided over the streets.

"You say this lil nigga is wild, right?" Lafayette asked, looking back and forth between the windshield and his Main Man.

"Yeah, Mayo is out there, but he respects my gangsta."

"Well, I don't know lil homie like that, so if he buck I'ma act an ass."

From the corner of his eye, Gar watched his homeboy pull his .9mm automatic from between the seat and lay it on his lap.

"You don't have to worry about that, the lil homie know what's up with me."

"I'm sure he does, but having my baby nearby makes me feel better."

"Bang this left on 35th street."

Lafayette made a left on 35th street and coasted down the residential block. He stopped at the center of the block at Gar's request. They were in front of a raggedy white house with a rusty gate and dirt for a front lawn. Posted at the bottom step was two young men shooting the shit and passing a blunt between them. They seemed to be ignorant of Lafayette and Gar's presence.

"Is that Black Face over there?" Gar asked no one in particular as he tried to peer through the darkness. "That is him." he answered his own question. He then yelled out of the window. "Yo, Black Face, is that nigga Mayo over here?"

"Who dat?" Black Face asked, tapping his homeboy. His homeboy went over into the bushes and retrieved something. Gar believed it was a banger.

"It's Gar, Blood."

"Bleed, that's the homie." Black Face told his homeboy, who'd recovered the banger and was now stashing it in the front of his Dickie shorts. Black Face turned to Gar yelling, "What it two, my nigga?"

"Mayo in there? I need to holla at 'em."

"Yeah, hold on." He ducked off inside of the house. A moment later, a tall nigga with an athletic physique emerged in a red beanie and red long sleeve Pro-Club. He carried his six foot two frame over to the passenger side of Lafayette's rental where Gar resided.

"What's up, Duce Owe?" he greeted Gar with a complex handshake.

For the first time Lafayette got a good look at the kid. He was pale in complexion, nearly as white as snow. He had dark brown eyes and long sandy brown hair, which he kept in six big cornrows. Though the youngster was barely seventeen, he held the appearance of a 30 year old man.

"Ain't shit, what y'all niggaz doing up in there?" Gar asked him.

"Nothing much, tryna freak off with these rats."

"My bad, my young nigga, didn't mean to pull you out of no pussy."

"Ah, don't even worry about them hoes, blood. It's bros over hoes this way."

"All day," Gar nodded. "What's up with your people, though?"

"Who dat?"

"Ya boy Zay," Gar answered. "I ain't seen'em in the hood in a minute. I heard he been out for a while."

"He's good. What chu asking about him for?" When Mayo saw Lafayette with the .9mm on his lap, he instinctively pulled the Glock .50 from his hip and pointed it at him. At that moment, Lafayette and Mayo had their bangers trained on one another, with Gar in the cross-hairs.

"Hold up now, what the hell is this?" Gar asked Mayo, looking between his homies.

"You tell me, fuck this nigga gotta strap out for?" Mayo mad dogged Lafayette, biting down on his bottom lip. He had both of his hands on the Glock, like he was a police officer and shit.

"We just came through here to talk." Lafayette told him the truth.

"It doesn't look like y'all came through here to talk to me."

Gar turned to his Main Man. "Put the gun down, La, and let me holla at the lil homie."

"I ain't putting shit down; you tell that young ass nigga to put his shit down."

"Not gone happen, Hhomes, I'll die for mine, I'ma young nigga who don't have shit to lose…besides my freedom."

"La, put the banger up, I'ma holla at this nigga and find out where Zay is." Gar spoke to him in a hushed tone. "Trust me, just like I trust you. He ain't gone do nothing 'cause I'll put fire to'em."

Lafayette blew hard and put his 9 Double M away. Mayo put his gun away and stepped back from the car, keeping his eyes on the hustler that had drawn down on him. Gar hopped out of the rental and slammed the door closed.

Black Face and his homeboy came walking up.

"What's happening, blood, you one hunnit?" he asked with furrowed brows.

"Y.G, good," Gar draped his arm over Mayo's shoulders and moved to walk up the block. "I just need to holla at'em for a few ticks." With that said, Black Face and his homeboy headed back into the yard while Gar and Mayo strode down the sidewalk.

"What chu won't with Zay, blood?" Mayo's forehead creased.

"Dig this, I'ma keep it one thousand with chu," Gar began, "Your people took us for some shit. We're just tryna get it back."

"You mean you tryna kill'em." Mayo looked him dead in his eyes.

"Fuck it," Gar took his arm from around the young boy's shoulders. "I don't know what I was thinking, you aren't green. You know how I get down. A nigga take what's mine and I take his life." He said with a scowl, putting it out there. If Mayo bucked then he was gone leave him leaking right there on 35th street.

Mayo massaged his chin as he thought on it. "Check it, I can tell you right where to find homie, but chu gotta make it worth my while."

"What chu won't?"

"I heard y'all slanging them thangs down by the way, gimmie a nice price on one of'em. I'm tryna step my game up out here."

"Let me holla at my nigga, and I'll see what we can do. Follow me," Gar motioned for Mayo to follow him as he headed back to the rental.

Gar stuck his head into the driver side window and swapped a few words with Lafayette. He stepped back and the driver side door opened. Lafayette hopped out and came around the rental. He stepped upon the curb where Mayo was posted up.

"How many birds you tryna score?" Lafayette asked.

"One."

"Just one?"

"Yeah, just one, I'm tryna get on my feet."

Lafayette thought to back when he was trying to step his game up and Shameek blessed him. He figured someone had given him a shot so it was only right that he did the same for someone else. It would be his way of honoring the memory of his old plug.

"Gimmie thirty."

"For one?"

"For one." He nodded.

"Shit, that's love." A smile stretched across Mayo's face for the first time. He slapped hands with Lafayette.

"When you get cho money up holla at Gar," Lafayette told him. "Now, your people address."

"Right," Mayo shot him Zay's address and he burned it on the wall inside of his memory bank. "All right, to satisfy my curiosity, what compelled you to give up your folks like that? Blood is thicker than water."

"Zay ain't my family." Mayo informed him. "He's my step father. He was married to my mom's. Shit, they still are married. They're just separated. Back in the day my uncle use to get money. I have reason to believe that it was Zay that robbed and killed him." He took the time to spit on the side-walk. "Only reason why I know where he stay is 'cause my lil Mexican bitch stay next door to 'em. Fuck that nigga, he ain't never done me no good, no way."

"All right, my nigga, good looking out." Lafayette dapped him up and headed for the rental. "Get at me when you ready for that."

"Shit, I'm ready now."

"Well, holla at Gar tomorrow then, he'll get chu right."

Lafayette hopped behind the wheel and pulled off. While the rental was in motion, Gar stuck his hand out of the window and threw up his hood. Mayo threw it back up at him and dipped off into the yard.

"So what's up, La? You tryna give this nigga his memorial tonight?" Gar asked.

"Nah, we'll get'em tomorrow night. I need to lay it down and get my head right, know what I'm saying?"

"No doubt," Gar's cell phone vibrated inside of his pocket. He dipped his hand into his Levi's and pulled it out. He checked the screen and saw that it was a "Blocked Number." He wasn't going to answer it at first, but his curiosity got the best of him. "Who dis?" he answered the cellular. "Yeah, this is him…all right. Yeah, I'll be there in a minute." He ended the call.

"What's up?"

"That was the hospital; Batice died."

"I'm sorry to hear that, fam." He took his hand off of the steering-wheel and gripped his shoulder affectionately.

"Yeah, me too,"Gar looked out of the passenger side window. He then said under his breath, "Fuck that bitch."

Chapter Eleven

Jason drove into a pitch black alley and killed the engine of his Mercedes. He snatched the briefcase off the passenger seat and opened the driver side door. He stepped out of his vehicle, one black leather Ferragamo shoe at a time. Afterwards, he closed the door and pulled out a slip of paper from his suit's jacket.

"I know this can't be the place." Jason said before reading over the address on the slip of paper. "This is it." his eyebrows raised, like he found it hard to believe that this was the location that his meeting was to take place. Coming to the conclusion that this was indeed the spot he was suppose to meet the nigga he'd spoken over the telephone with, he shrugged and tucked the slip of paper back inside of his suit's jacket. Next, he trekked through the alley, observing his surroundings and looking for the man he was supposed to meet. Hearing an empty can hit the wet ground inside of the alley; Jason swung around, and in one swift motion, drew his chrome .357 Magnum revolver. He spotted an empty peaches can and a stray cat running off.

"Scare easily, don't we?" a voice came from Jason's rear. He whipped around ready to let his thang off and came across a mysterious man in a big hat and a black leather duster. The darkness of the alley hid his face and not even the movements of his lips could be seen. Though Jason couldn't make out his eyes he could feel their intensity. It was as if they peered straight through him and into his soul.

"Do me a favor and put the gun away, those things make me edgy."

The lawyer shoved the pistol back inside of the holster on his hip.

"Sorry about that." Jason apologized and pushed his glasses back upon his nose.

"Now, I understand that you acquire my services." The mysterious man said. "Who's this hemorrhoid you need removed from your ass?"

"My wife."

Jason had hired a private investigator to dig up any dirt he could find on Montrice. During the P.I's investigation he found out Montrice was seeing a young man by the name of Lafayette Myers. He brought him footage of Montrice and Lafayette having sex. When Jason saw the footage he wasn't the least bit surprised. It only confirmed his suspicions of his wife's infidelity.

Jason thought he heard Montrice scream out Lafayette's name the day he'd caught her masturbating in their bed. But she told him that he was mistaken. Now he had found out that he had heard right. On top of that, he believed that she was pregnant. As of late, she'd been craving strange food and throwing up. Jason wasn't a hundred percent sure, but he had a gut feeling about it. The sad part about it was there was no way that it was his. Unbeknownst to Montrice, he had gotten a vasectomy a few years before he'd met her, because he didn't want to have kids. He knew how much she wanted children and thought that if he told her she would have never married him.

Montrice's affair had left Jason crushed. He was devastated by her betrayal. He couldn't believe that she would play him like that. At first he grieved but that grief grew into an ugly hatred. Sometimes at night when he'd be lying next to her in bed, he'd think about suffocating her with his pillow. He believed that her death would be the only thing that would make him feel better, but he knew that his hands would have to be clean of it. He'd be the first person the police would suspect being that he was her husband. He decided that he'd be better off hiring someone to do the deed while he went off somewhere with plenty of people and cameras for his alibi.

"Ah, old lady's fucking around, huh?" the mysterious man said. "Not to worry, I'll take care of her. I'll assume that you've been informed of my rate."

"Yes, I have your money right here." Jason handed him the briefcase.

The mysterious man's gloved hand reached out and grasped the handle of the briefcase, lowering it to his side. He didn't even bother to pop the locks and count the money.

"Her photograph, her work schedule and the license plate number of her car are all inside."

"I got cha, champ, all I need is forty-eight hours and you'll be a widower."

Rustling at Jason's rear drew his attention. He turned around and saw an old homeless man fishing around inside of the trash bin. When he turned back around the mysterious man had vanished. All that was left was a thick fog that seemed to roll back into the depths of the dark alley. Jason scratched his head and looked around. Shrugging his shoulders, he hopped back inside of his whip and drove off.

***

Loon and Theo sat inside of a navy blue Chevy Tahoe listening to 50 cent's *Don't push me,* passing an L and sipping dark liquor from plastic cups. Everyone's eyes were low, except for C-Bo's; he was sitting in the backseat. Homie didn't drink or get high. It just wasn't his thing. He believed that liquor and marijuana clouded your judgment. And he preferred a clean and sober mind.

Theo shook his head. "I tried to push her death to the back of my mind, but somehow she keeps coming up. I see her when I'm out in the streets and I have nightmares about her. I be waking up in cold sweats and shit…shaking like Muhammad Ali. Sometimes I think I'ma go crazy, cuzzo. It's like this broad is haunting me. The only time I'm all right is when I'm high. I can't do the sober dance. I'd go fucking insane." He took a pull from the L and tried to pass it to Loon but he waved him off. He then mashed the blunt out into the ashtray and took a sip of his drink.

"I feel you, man." Loon began. "I've been kind of fucked up over the shit, too. Especially since that baby was involved. My conscience has been eating away at me, loc. I mean, I done slumped niggaz before and didn't feel shit. But this shit," he shook his head and pressed on, "this shit is different. I've been seriously thinking about turning myself in. What do you think?" he sat his plastic cup into the cup-holder after taking a sip.

"I've been thinking about the same shit, too. I just didn't come at chu with it 'cause I didn't know how you would react.

I think that's the best thing for us to do, if we ever hope to come to be able to live with ourselves."

"Well, shit, when are you tryna roll up to the station?"

"We can go in the A.M, 'cause tonight I'm tryna get stupid, dumb high. Feel me?"

"Yep," Loon gave C-Bo a look through the rear-view mirror and stared out of the driver side window. He closed his eyes and massaged the bridge of his nose, "Weak ass mothafucka."

C-Bo slipped a length of fishing line around Theo's neck and pulled back, tightening it around his throat and cutting off his oxygen. Theo dropped his cup of liquor and it splashed at his feet on the floor. He tried to slip his fingers under the fishing line but it was just too tight around his neck. His eyes bugged, turning glassy and red. His mouth dropped open and he gagged, tongue moving around wildly. His eyes welled up with tears and spilled down his cheeks. Theo's back arched as he rose up in the passenger seat on the tips of his sneakers, grunting and choking. Suddenly, his legs thrashed around. He tried to claw his executioner's hands, but they were gloved. C-Bo pulled the fishing line even tighter around that hoe ass nigga'z neck, adding the pressure of all of his weight. Beads of sweat formed on C-Bo's forehead and rolled down his face. The armpits of his T-shirt darkened from perspiration. His face twisted and he clenched his teeth, straining. Theo's struggling grew weaker by the second until he eventually went limp. His eyes stared out of their corners and his tongue hung out the side of his mouth. He was dead.

When C-Bo slipped the length of fishing line from around his victim's throat, there was a red ring around his neck. Exhausted, the nigga lay back in his seat with his head tilted back breathing hard, his chest heaving up and down. He wiped the sweat from his forehead with the back of his gloved hand.

"Dawg, I thought this mothafucka was gone never die." C-Bo said.

Loon leaned over and held two fingers to Theo's neck, checking his pulse. "Yeah, this mothafucka gone," He confirmed and slapped a baseball cap on Theo's head, tilting it down to cover up his face. He did this because he wanted to make it look like his dead ass was asleep. "Yo dump this nigga and burn this mothafucka up." He referred to the Tahoe truck. "Bang my burnout when you're finished and I'll send Big Sam to come get chu."

"All right," C-Bo said from the backseat. He swung open the backseat door and hopped out of the truck, making his way around to the other side of the SUV.

Loon pulled out a rag and wiped down everything he'd touched inside of the truck. He then used the rag to open the driver side door and hopped out. He dapped up C-Bo and went on about his business. The executioner slid in behind the wheel of the Tahoe, fired that big bastard up and drove off.

***

"That's $375,000 dollars." Zay counted the last of the money they'd gotten from kicking in niggaz doors. "We keep coming off with licks like this here and we'll have a mill ticket in no time." He picked up his glass of dark brown liquor and lay back on the brown leather couch. La'Chat lay sprawled on the couch, snuggled under his arm. She intertwined her fingers with his and used her other hand to caress his bulging bicep. He'd been in a fire when he was a eighteen. His hands had gotten burned badly and looked like beef jerky. They had a funny texture too, but La'Chat didn't seem to mind.

"Don't forget we still have those six blocks we gotta fence." La'Chat reminded him as she lovingly kissed his hideously burned hand.

"That's spoken for already, babe." He told her. "I gotta cat that's willing to take 'em all off of our hands."

"How much are we gone let 'em get 'em for?" she looked up at him.

"I told 'em fifteen a piece, that's a deal too sweet to turn down." He leaned forth and sat his glass of dark brown liquor on the coffee-table. "Hell, I 'ma see if I can pawn those pounds of Kush we got on 'em, too."

"Why not just take 'em for the loot and keep our shit?"

"You're talking about a double cross, huh? As much as I'd love to, I can't. Homes is the brotha of a good buddy of mine from back in the day. Dude saved me from getting my shit pushed in up at Delano. I was just a tall, skinny snot nosed kid. Cat didn't know me, nor did he owe me shit, but he helped keep them niggaz off my black ass. He's got my love and respect, so I gotta be on the up and up on this one."

"Square biz, huh?"

"Square biz." He nodded.

La'Chat sat up on the couch, facing him and studying his brown eyes. "I love you, Zay." She caressed his cheek.

"I love you too, baby." He leaned forth and stuck his tongue inside of her mouth. Their tongues intertwined and their mouths engulfed one another's. They kissed passionately and hard. Zay leaned her back, kissing her along the way. She helped him slip his wife-beater over his head and she removed her bra. Her fingers busied themselves unbuckling his belt and unzipping his jeans, while his was unbuttoning hers and unzipping them. A split second later, he was sliding his thick, long dick into her shaved twat. Sensual cries filled the living room as Zay gave his soul mate that Thug Passion.

Chapter Twelve

It was early in the morning and Gar found himself at Batice's auntie's door, wearing a long face and ringing the doorbell. As soon as the middle aged woman opened the door and allowed him entrance into her home, he started with the wet works and broke out into a performance that would have gotten him nominated for several Academy Awards.

"I just can't believe she's gone, you know?" Gar sobbed behind red eyes and a tear stained face. "I had big plans for us, real big plans. After she got outta rehab and had gotten herself together…I'd planned to propose to her. I had gotten the ring and everything. See," he pulled a small red velvet box from out of his pocket and opened it. It boasted a four carat diamond, platinum engagement ring. It was beautiful, absolutely stunning.

"Oh, Clarence," Batice's aunty said with her hands over her mouth and her face slick with tears. She had raised Batice as well as a host of other nephews and nieces that affectionately called her, Momma. "Come here." She opened her arms. Gar closed the red velvet box and embraced his baby momma's aunty, sobbing and hollering. He quieted down for a moment and listened to her cries. He sighed and rolled his eyes, hearing her wailing. She broke their embrace and held on to his hands, staring into his eyes. "In time things will get better, you've just gotta be strong for you and Lil Gar, OK?"

Gar nodded as he wiped his eyes with the back of his hand.

"I know, I know, Shirley," he replied. "Well, listen; I gotta go make these funeral arrangements. I'll call you once everything is set in Chrome with the time and place of the proceedings." He took the Kleenex she gave him and dabbed his tear streaked face.

"Would you like me to come with you?"

"Oh no, Shirley, I couldn't burden you."

"It's notta burden, baby, we're family. We've got to get through this tragedy together."

"OK." He nodded in agreement. "But let's do this tomorrow instead."

Shirley rubbed his back as she led him to the door and opened it.

"You just call me when you're ready to go, OK, baby?" she hugged him once more at the door. Over her shoulder he could see her big round booty in the egg shaped mirror behind her. *Damn, she gotta fat ass,* he mouthed before breaking their embrace and hustling down the steps. He walked to the car dabbing his eyes dry with the Kleenex. He snatched open the door of Lafayette's rental and waved goodbye to Shirley. Once she had waved back and closed the door, he slid in behind the wheel and fired up the engine.

"Edward Norton eat cho mothafucking heart out." He tossed the balled up Kleenex aside and drove off, wearing a wicked smile.

***

Montrice sat on the toilet with her panties around her ankles. She wore a stunned expression on her face and had a pregnancy test stick in her hand. The stick had a blue plus sign which meant that she was indeed with child. She couldn't believe it. Her eyes were bugged and her mouth was wide open. She looked to the stick again. Not believing the results, she shook the stick up, but the plus sign wouldn't disappear. She held her hands to her face and sobbed as quietly as she could, so Jason wouldn't hear her.

Once Montrice had finished crying, she wiped her eyes with the back of her hands. She rose from off the toilet seat, wiped herself and dumped the tissue paper into the commode. Next, she pulled up her panties and tossed the pregnancy test stick into the commode, flushing it down. Having done this, she turned on the water and washed her hands under the flowing water. She splashed water onto her face and used a bath towel to dry her face. She then pulled her hair back into a ponytail. She took a step towards the bathroom door and grabbed the knob. Afterwards, she took a deep breath before pulling the door open and stepping out into the bedroom.

Jason lay with one leg hanging off the side of the bed, fully dressed in a suit. His hands were nestled at his waist and he was snoring aloud. The flat-screen was still on and *Family Matters* played on the "42 inch screen. Montrice picked up her purse and grabbed her banger from out of the nightstand drawer. She kissed her husband on the forehead and left the bedroom. She was on her way to break the news to Lafayette.

***

Lafayette paced the floor on his cell phone listening to it ring and occasionally glancing at his G-Shock. Diana stared up at him from where she sat at the kitchen table, repackaging a block of cocaine that she'd just finished stretching into two. Though her hands were busy her eyes were watching Lafayette closely. Once she was done repackaging the block of cocaine, Diana picked it up from the table and slid it inside of a big brown paper bag with Ralph's emblazoned on the front of it.

Diana rolled the brown paper bag down and handed it to Lafayette, giving him a less than friendly expression. Lafayette took the brown paper bag from her and made a mental note of how she and Auntie were acting.

"Ms. Dickey? Yeah, this is Lafayette. How are you?" he said into his cellular once Lil Man's mother had picked up. "Good. Oh, I'm straight, taking it one day at a time, you know? Well, listen, I was going to come by there to drop off the money for Anthony's ceremony." He listened to what she was saying before replying. "OK, well, I should be by there in about an hour. All right, bye." He ended the call and peeked through the blinds. Gar had just pulled up in front of the trap. Lafayette turned around to one of his newest recruits. "Yo, Naughty, hold it down, my nigga. I'm outro."

"Don't worry about nothing, La, I got chu faded." Naughty said, buckling his belt. He'd just come out of the bathroom from taking a shit. He snatched up a chair and planted it in the corner of the kitchen so he could keep a good eye on the old women and the product.

Lafayette closed the door behind him as he stepped out onto the porch. He hustled down the steps with his package tucked snuggly under his arm. Walking across the lawn, he saw Montrice approaching. Her eyes were red and puffy and she was holding herself. Lafayette raised an eyebrow, wondering what had happened with her. The first thing he thought was that her husband had found out about them.

"Lafayette, I need to talk to you." Montrice said as he came out of the yard.

He glanced at his G-Shock and said, "Make it quick, I gotta bend a few corners."

Montrice looked away trying to find the courage to say what was on her mind. She blew hard and decided to throw caution to the wind.

"I'm pregnant." She blurted, putting it out there.

"Congratulations." He said, brushing past her.

Montrice grabbed him by his arm and turned him around.

"Lafayette, it's yours. I know because Jason and I haven't been intimate up 'til a couple of weeks ago."

"OK. You're pregnant and I'm the father. What do you want me to do?"

Montrice opened her mouth to say something but nothing came out. She was choked up. "Showing a little moral support would be nice." She said, wiping the lone tear that trickled down her cheek. "It's your child, too."

"You're right, my bad." He dipped his hand into his pocket and pulled out a wad of bills. He licked his thumb and made to peel off a few dead presidents. "How much is the abortion going to cost?" A stunned expression captured Montrice's face and her mouth dropped open. She was appalled that he would even suggest such an idea. "Wait a minute, I'm tripping. You're a cop. You have health insurance. It covers that, right?" he stuck the wad of bills back into his pocket.

"You fucking asshole!" Montrice started punching on Lafayette, causing him to drop his package. He grabbed her by the wrists and forced her onto the hood of an old sky blue Chevy Malibu. Seeing this, Gar threw open the door of the rental and stepped a foot out onto the street.

"Bitch, what the fuck is your problem?" Lafayette barked, raining spittle in her face. "You already knew what it was with us! I'm not tryna start no family with chu or nan other hoe! I'm married to these streets, and I'm not about to have no mothafucking affair!" he released her wrists and scooped up his package, keeping his hateful eyes on her.

Montrice got up off the hood of the Chevy Malibu. She couldn't stop the tears from cascading down her face.

"So it's like that now? You're just gonna abandon me and your baby?"

"How many months are you?"

"I don't know. A couple of weeks, I guess." She wiped her eyes.

"Good. That means it isn't a baby yet. You still got time to take care of that."

"You bastard," Montrice's face twisted into something demon like. Her eyes exploded with fire and she clenched her teeth, boasting the skeletal structure of her jaws. She dipped her hand inside of her purse and pulled out her banger. She gripped the steel with both hands and pointed it at the man she was sucking and fucking behind her husband's back. Gar drew one of his .45s and pointed it at Montrice. "I should blow your fucking black heart out!"

Lafayette placed his package on the hood of the rental and motioned for Gar to put his gun away. "It's cool, Gar, I got it." Gar heard what his Main Man said, but he still kept his heater trained on Montrice. Lafayette slowly approached Montrice with both of his hands raised in the air.

"Don't come any closer La, or I swear to God I'll shoot chu dead!" she swore, looking his ass dead in the eyes. Little momma had a firm grasp on her weapon and her finger was ready to squeeze off a kill-shot.

"You want to kill me? Go right ahead." He told her as he approached, cautiously. "Your son or daughter will grow up without a father. How are you going to explain to them that you were the one that stole me away from them? How are you going to do that, huh?" he looked at her with glassy eyes that seemed to beg for lenience.

Montrice took one hand away from her weapon to wipe the tears from her face, but quickly grasped it back.

"It isn't like you care about them anyway." She said, sniffling.

"You sure about that? Maybe it's just that I don't want him or her to have a father like me. What would it be like? Me running the streets all of the time and barely being home to see'em? It'll be as good as not having a father at all."

"No." she shook her head. "You could leave this life. I have plenty of money for us to move away and start up a business of our own."

"Is that what chu want? For us to settle down and raise a family?" Montrice nodded yes. By this time, Lafayette was about three feet away from her. "OK then, give me the gun and we can talk this out. I'll have Gar handle my affairs for me so we can chop it up about how we gonna raise our baby." He slowly reached in to take the banger from her hands.

"OK." She nodded, allowing him to slip the weapon from out of her hands.

Once Lafayette had the banger in his hand, he sighed with relief and then punched Montrice dead in her mouth. She hit the sidewalk with a thud, grimacing and bleeding at mouth. "The next time you point a strap at me, you better use it, hoe!" he stomped her in the stomach, not giving a fuck that she was pregnant with his baby. Montrice's back lifted from the concrete as she hugged her stomach. She sobbed aloud.

"Stupid ass bitch!" Lafayette pressed a button that ejected the fully loaded magazine. The magazine slipped out of the bottom of the weapon and hit the ground; he kicked it off of the curb. He then wiped his finger prints off of the gun, dropped it into the street and kicked it into the storm drain. Afterwards, he snatched his package off the hood of the rental and gave Montrice one last look before hopping into the passenger seat. Gar fired up the rental and pulled off, leaving homegirl sobbing and staining the sidewalk with her teardrops.

Chapter Thirteen

"So what chu gone do about that sitch (situation)?" Gar looked both ways before making a right turn.

"What chu mean? I'm out here, nigga, I'm devoted to this here." Lafayette spoke on his occupation in the streets.

"I know. But I know you're not gonna be no deadbeat. I know you're not going out like that, are you?"

"Nah, I'ma kick her down for mine, but as far as me being involved like that…fuck nah. I'm on my get money tip."

"Man…and they say I'ma cold nigga." He pulled into the parking lot of a liquor store on Jefferson. Moments later, a silver Envoy truck pulled into the parking space beside him. Behind the wheel sat Black Face. He threw his head back like *What's up?* Gar returned the gesture. The passenger side door swung opened and Mayo jumped down to the pavement. He made his way around the enormous truck and hopped into the backseat of Lafayette's rental. The trio exchanged *'What's ups?'* and then he passed Lafayette a brown paper bag full of dirty money.

"That's thirty bands, my nigga." Mayo said. "I'll kick it 'til you finish counting it up."

"My right-hand vouched for you, you're good money." Lafayette assured him.

"Bool." The young nigga touched fists with Gar and Lafayette before hopping out of the backseat. He climbed back into the silver Envoy. The enormous truck pulled out of the parking lot and into traffic, the volume rising on some rap music.

"Where are we off to now? Lil Man's momma's crib?" Gar inquired.

"Yeah, I gotta drop this paper off for this ceremony. She supposed to be getting 'em cremated but I'ma let her have the rest of them few grips. I know she's not gonna feel like going to work and shit. Hell, her son just got murdered."

"You want me to handle it for you?"

"Nah, I'ma take care of it."

"All right," Gar fired up the rental and threw the car in reverse. He made to back out and a black Lincoln Town Car pulled up behind him. "What the fuck?"

Lafayette looked into the rear-view mirror. He saw the driver side door of the limousine open and Ren emerge, buttoning a button on his suit. He made his way around the vehicle and approached the passenger side of the rental where Lafayette resided. He then stooped down to the window and Lafayette held down the button on the door panel, letting the window down.

"What's cracking, Ren?" he asked.

"I can't call it." the big man responded. "Look here, boss lady wants you to take a ride with her."

Lafayette shook his head. "No can do, big man, I gotta lotta corners I gotta bend today."

"Lafayette, man, you really wanna take this ride, trust me." Ren looked him in his eyes wearing a serious expression.

Lafayette shook his head no. He was about to open his mouth with a response, when Gar spoke over him. "Look, La, gone and see what old girl wants, I can take care of the rest of the business for the day."

The hustler took a deep breath and said, "You sure?"

Gar nodded yes.

"What about that other thang?"

"I got all bases cover, blood. Trust me. That's why you put me on the team."

"All right," Lafayette dapped him up and hopped out of the rental.

Through the rear-view mirror, Gar watched as Lafayette followed Ren to the limousine. The big man opened the back door for the hustler. Once he slid inside, homeboy closed the door and hustled over to the driver side. He hopped in behind the wheel and pulled out of the parking lot.

"What is this all about?" Lafayette asked Victoria, taking in her hairstyle and attire. Her hair was pulled back in a simple ponytail. She wore a black turtle neck, olive green cargo pants and combat boots. This was the first time he hadn't seen her all dressed up.

Victoria swallowed the last of the champagne in her flute and sat it down. She then picked up the folded manila envelope beside her and passed it to him. Lafayette opened the manila envelope and pulled out a deck of black and white photographs. He sat the envelope aside and went through the photographs. Victoria watched him attentively as she took pulls from a joint, polluting the confines of the limousine with white smoke.

"Those photos are of Diablo Sanchez's capos and most of his soldiers." She informed Lafayette. "Diablo managed to escape, but not before one of my men popped a cap in his brown ass. Don't worry, we'll get him; he's probably laid up in some shitty Mexican hospital, if he is my guys will find him. I have a band of some of the best trained mercenaries there are scouring Mexico as we speak. They'll eat that spic alive." She assured him.

Lafayette nodded. He finished looking through the photographs, dropped them into the manila envelope and handed them back to her.

"The Sanchez Cartel has been crippled, and soon their reign will be no more." She swore. "I promise you that."

"Well, I hope you stand by your words, 'cause I'm going to hold you to them."

"As expected."

"Where are we headed now?"

"Lafayette, please, sit back, relax and enjoy the ride." She opened her gold case and held it out towards to him. He picked out one of the neatly rolled joints and slipped it between his lips. She took the liberty to fire it up with her trusty Zippo-lighter. He lay back in his seat taking pulls from the Jay, while she activated the stereo with a compact remote control. Rick Ross feat Wiz Khalifa *'I stay high'* ripped through the speakers of the limousine.

That night

Loon coasted through the streets under the influence of O.G Kush. His eyes were as slanted as Lucy Liu's and he wore a silly expression on his face. On his passenger side was one of his boys, Chrome, taking pulls from a blunt so thick it was bursting at the seams with weed. In the backseat sat their latest conquests, two identical chocolate twins with breasts that were threatening to spill out of their matching form fitting dresses. The women were equally gorgeous. The only way they could be told apart was from their different hairstyles.

The twins were just as faded as Loon and Chrome. Only their poison of choice was a bottle of Remy Martin. They laughed and cackled with the men as they indulged in the dark liquor.

"Yo, I'm tryna hit some of that Remy," Loon looked up into the rear-view mirror at the twin with the long, silky flat-ironed hair. "Po' up," He told her.

Flat-ironed hair had just poured the last of the Remy into her plastic cup. "Uh oh, it looks like we're all out, gotta make a store run."

"Loon, pull over to that all night joint right there." Chrome pointed across from Loon to a 24 hour liquor store.

He nodded and said, "All right."

Loon pulled into the parking lot of the 24 hour liquor store. He killed the engine and he and Chrome hopped out of the Land Rover. They made their way towards the store while the twins stayed behind inside of the truck. A bell chimed as Loon and Chrome crossed the threshold into the store. Loon locked eyes with a tall, bronze skinned dude in a black Chicago Bulls beanie and matching sweatshirt, who was making his way out of the store. The two men held one another's gaze for a split second, but that's all it took for a light bulb of recognition to come on inside of Loon's head. Loon's forehead wrinkled remembering the man's face, but he couldn't recall where he knew him from. He shrugged and went about his business. Once he and Chrome purchased their items, they made their way out of the liquor store.

"My nigga, Chrome, are you ready to tag team both of these hoes?" Loon smiled, chewing on a red licorice.

"You mothafucking right," A smile stretched across Chrome's face as he shook the black box of Magnums in his hand.

Automatic gunfire ripped through the air, and with it came Chrome's bugged eyes and roars of pain. His shirt looked like he got hit with a barrage of rotten tomatoes as he went plummeting to the sidewalk. A shocked expression surfaced on Loon's face as he watched his boy get cut down. He looked up and saw the dude he'd passed on his way into the store running towards him. The lower half of the bronze skinned dude's face was covered by a dingy white T-shirt and he was gripping a Tec-9 with both hands. Loon went to grab his thang from his hip and snatched air. That's when he remembered that he left his banger in the stash spot inside of his Land Rover. He turned to run and got about four feet before his calf and thigh exploded with fire. Before he knew it the ground came slamming into his face, bloodying his grill and loosening his front teeth. Loon was in excruciating pain, but knew he had to get away if he wanted to live to see another sunrise. He crawled down the pavement trying to pull his limp leg along, but his attempts at escape where useless. The bronze skinned dude ran upon him and pulled him over onto his back by the collar of his shirt. Loon grimaced feeling the fire engulfing his wounded leg, but pushed the thoughts of pain to the back of his brain once he saw a pair of evil eyes staring down at him. The bronze skinned dude pulled the dingy T-shirt down from the lower half of his face, revealing his identity.

"That was my family you blasted on in that Magnum that night, cock sucka!" Gar growled angrily.

Loon saw the tattoo on Gar's neck advertising his hood, Eastside Rolling 20s Bloods. Laughing manically, he said, "Yeah? Ask me do I give a fuck?"

"Oh, that's funny? Well, you should really get a kick out of this." He stuck the hollowed barrel of the Tec-9 into that mothafucka'z grill and squeezed his eye shut, pulling the trigger. Gar expected homie's dome to explode, but strangely nothing happened. He looked to the semi-automatic weapon and saw that it was jammed by a shell.

"Fuck!" Gar scowled. He took the Tec-9 from his victim's grill and tried to un-jam it. Seeing his assailant struggle with the weapon, Loon continued to laugh manically. His long and hard laughter angered him. Gar pulled Loon to his eye level by the front of his shirt. He then gripped the Tec-9 as tight as he could and cracked him in the face repeatedly with it. Once Loon's face was a bloody mess and he was groaning in pain, Gar let his body hit the pavement. He then ran off, pulling the white T-shirt over the lower half of his face. The nigga ran into the liquor store parking lot and came across the chocolate twins. He pointed his Tec-9 at them and barked, "Don't fucking look at me!" the twins screamed and their hands shot up into the air, trembling. Still holding his Tec-9 on them, Gar slowly backed away from them and opened the door of his rental. He hopped into his vehicle and sped out of the liquor store's parking lot.

***

Lafayette surveyed his surroundings as the limousine pulled up outside of an abandoned toy factory. Ren came to the back of the vehicle and snatched open the backdoor. Once Lafayette and Victoria un-boarded the limousine, Ren closed the door and led them to the shutter of the warehouse. He knocked on the shutter in a specific pattern before it was pulled upward. On the opposite side stood a tall, dark skinned brother in black fatigues and cap. A black bandana was around his neck, cowboy style. An M-16 assault rifle was slung around his back. His brows formed a slight scowl and his lips were a straight line. His eyes scanned over the trio before stepping aside and allowing them to enter.

Lafayette ducked under the shutter and came in behind Victoria and Ren. He scanned the warehouse. It was empty and spacious. At the center of the abandoned tenement was a cluster of men, all dressed in black fatigues and caps, gripping their respective weapons. Lafayette gathered that these were the same men that crushed The Sanchez Cartel. Approaching the fold, Lafayette saw that the men were surrounding two people, both of whom were on their knees with black pillow cases over their heads. Once the hustler was upon them he could tell that one was a man and the other was a woman, by the clothes they wore.

The black fatigue clad men parted and allowed Victoria into their circle. She wore a serious expression on her face as she stepped behind the captures. One by one, she yanked the black pillowcases from the heads of the man and woman, revealing their identities. The man and woman were Garza and Isabella Sanchez. Isabella's eyes bored into Lafayette's scowling face. Her teeth were clenched and her jaws were tight. She was mad dogging him, looking like she was ready to gouge out his eyes. She looked around at all of the black fatigue clad men, spitting something mean and nasty in Spanish at them.

"Nothing more fierce than a ticked off Spanish mami." One of the men said, harping up a nasty glob and spitting off to the side.

"Try a pissed off sista." Victoria challenged, eyebrows arched and nose scrunched up. For the first time Lafayette noticed the metal baseball bat slung over her shoulder. It seemed like the metal bat had magically appeared in her hand. He could have sworn that she hadn't had it a minute ago.

"P…please, just let me and my sister go," Garza pleaded. "I swear on my father's grave, you'll never see our faces again." He trembled with fear, looking up at the hustler. "Lafayette, please, I swear to God. It'll be as if we vanished from off the face of the earth."

"Jesus Christ." Victoria frowned and turned her head. A pungent odor had assaulted her nostrils. It had assaulted her men's nostrils as well, because they frowned and turned their heads too.

"Jesus Christ." One soldier stated, twisting his face up.

"Holy shit." Another one covered his nose and mouth.

"Fuck is that smell?" A third one asked.

Several of the soldiers turned their heads, not able to stand the overwhelming odor.

"He shit his pants," Victoria announced, pinching her nose.

Lafayette shook his head and chuckled. For all of the gangster shit Garza popped, inside he was as soft and as wet as a mothafucking Wet Wipe. He put on a Mafioso façade while in the company of his henchmen, but when faced with drama alone he folded like a bad hand in Poker. Lafayette couldn't believe that he used to look up to this man. He was truly ashamed of himself. If he could go back in time the things he would tell his younger self.

"I was going to have the fellas do'em in, but I decided to let chu do the honors." Victoria passed Lafayette the metal baseball bat.

Lafayette took the metal bat and brought it to the top of Isabella's head. She stared up into his eyes defiantly.

"If you expect me to beg for my life, you can kiss my skinny, brown ass." She harped up phlegm and spat it in his face. He closed his eyes tight just as the goo splattered against his face. He laughed and wiped his face with the back of his fist.

"I gotta tip my hat to you, bitch, you got more heart than your punk ass brotha." Lafayette told her with an amused expression. "That's why I'm not gone let chu go out like this bitch made ass nigga is!" he snatched the banger from the holster of the man standing beside him and pointed it at Isabella.

BLOCKA! BLOCKA! BLOCKA! BLOCKA! BLOCKA! BLOCKA!

Lafayette's weapon spat fast and furious, hollowing Isabella's chest and laying her on her back. She lay on the cold warehouse ground, her eyes blinking and her mouth gurgling blood. Lafayette stood over her squeezing the trigger of his banger relentlessly.

BLOCKA! BLOCKA! BLOCKA! BLOCKA!

Lafayette released the trigger and the barrel of his weapon wafted with white smoke. Isabella lay at his feet twisted. Her eyes bugged and her grill wide open. Specks of blood were on her neck and under her chin. Lafayette passed the banger back to the man he'd snatched it from. He then stepped to Garza with the metal baseball bat.

"Oh, my God, no," Garza wept as tears spilled down his cheeks. "My poor baby sister, I'm sorry. I'm so, so sorry!"

"Don't worry, mijo, you'll join her soon enough." Lafayette's assured him as he lifted the metal baseball bat above his head. Garza's punk ass sobbed and continued to beg for his life, staring up at the hustler. His entire form shivered all over as he waited for his execution. Lafayette stared down at the man that he hated with every inch of his heart. He brought the baseball bat down above his head several times, practicing his kill-strike. Garza shut his eyes and piss dripped from between his legs. He sniffled and his mouth quivered. Lafayette brought the baseball bat above his head one last time, and then he delivered the first blow.

CRACKKK!

CLIIING!

The baseball bat deflected off of that bitch ass nigga'z skull, cracking that mothafucka like an egg. The impact from the bat broke Garza's neck and left him lying awkwardly on the ground, neck twisted at a funny angle. The hustler slammed the metal baseball bat into that hoe ass nigga'z dome a second time, causing his eyeball to bulge out of his head. The third time caved his skull in and caused his body to spasm. Lafayette zoned out, slamming the bat into Garza's skull, repeatedly. He grunted, swinging the bat down with all of his might, gritting. Specks of blood clung to his sneakers and clothing. He looked like he was chopping a log with an axe. Once he was done he stood erect, admiring his handiwork and gripping the metal baseball bat. He smiled wickedly and wiped the specks of blood from off of his forehead with the back of his hand, breathing hard as hell. Garza's head resembled a crushed watermelon. What was left of his skull looked like chunks of raw burger and spaghetti sauce.

Lafayette took one last deep breath and tossed the baseball bat beside Garza's body. He then thanked Victoria and walked towards the outside, the men in the military garb parting like the Red Sea.

***

Gar couldn't believe his luck when he bumped into Loon on his way out of the liquor store. He damn near broke his neck running back to the rental. His adrenaline was pumping and his heart pounded, masking up with the dingy white T-shirt in the trunk and cocking the hammer on his Tec-9. He managed to lay down one of that nigga Loon's homies, and even gave Loon's bitch ass a couple. He had moved to finish him off but the Tec fucked around and jammed up on him. Gar chastised himself for not sticking with his trusty .45 automatic handguns. His babies always got the job done and had never jammed up on him. The Tec on the other hand always had a jamming problem.

Gar wasn't about to beat himself up too bad about missing his chance to slaughter Loon though. Los Angeles was but so big, so he was sure he'd run into him again. And when he did, he was gone give that ass the business.

Gar hopped out of the rental and made his way into the front-yard of the trap. His forehead wrinkled when he noticed that the lights were off. He glanced at the screen of his cell phone and wondered what the lights were doing off at that hour. The trap was normally jumping at that hour with activity. He found it strange that it was as dead as a limp dick.

Gar walked upon the porch and knocked on the front-door. He waited a while but no one answered. He tried to peek inside of the window, but the curtains were blocking his view. That's when he decided to walk around to the side of the house to try the side door. Once he was there he twisted the knob, and surprisingly the door opened. Once he'd stepped inside of the house, he flipped on the light switch but the lights didn't come on. He flipped the light switch on and off rapidly, but the lights still didn't come on. Gar dipped into the pocket of his Levi's and pulled out a Bic lighter. His thumb brushed down hard on the metal mechanism of the lighter and a flame was conceived, licking the air.

Gar made his way through the darkness with his lighter leading the way, its golden orange illumination shone on his face. When he came across something in the corner of the kitchen, he turned around. His forehead wrinkled when he saw Naughty sitting in the corner in a chair, his throat slit from ear to ear. A light shined on Gar's face from his right, blinding him. He whipped around and Auntie was holding a flashlight in his face with a gun extended underneath it. When Gar saw the handgun he dropped his lighter and broke for the side door, sneakers screeching on the linoleum floor.

152

BOC! BOC! BOC!

The first bullet slammed into Gar's chest causing him to howl in pain. A second one slammed into his shoulder as he made it to the doorway of the side door, dripping blood along the way. The third one splintered the wood of the doorway and sprayed debris everywhere. Gar had made it out of the door and was staggering down the walkway as fast as he could, holding his bleeding shoulder, blood oozed from between his fingers. He'd just made it to the front of the house when Diana appeared out of nowhere. Mad dogging him, she lifted her banger and squeezed the trigger. A bullet slammed into Gar's lower abdomen and doubled him over wincing. He staggered backwards. He tried to grab a hold of something to stop from falling, but ended up grabbing air. Gar fell to the ground on his back, staring up at the sky and breathing heavily. Auntie emerged from the doorway of the side door, clutching her banger in one hand and a flashlight in the other. She moved in to finish her victim off, leveling her banger between his eyes. Diana walked over and stood beside her, pointing her banger at Gar as well. Lying on his back, all he could see were the silhouettes of the women and the hollowed faces of their weapons.

Damn, I guess this is it, Gar thought, *I can't be mad though. I'm gone get it how I lived it. When it's all said and done, they're gonna bury me a G.*

BLOC!

A bullet shot through the back of Diana's neck and exited out of her face. Her body crashed to the ground making a nasty thud. Blood specks and chunks of brain fragments clung to the side of Auntie's face. Her eyes grew big and zoomed in on Lafayette. He charged forth, pulling the trigger of his banger. The weapon jumped in the palm of his hand, recoiling with every shot it spat. Auntie backed up, sending heat Lafayette's way. She managed to get off one shot before two hot-ones sizzled through the fabric of her light gray hoodie and melted into her chest. A shocked expression went across her face and she looked down where she was hit, seeing burgundy spots expanding where she was struck. She touched her wounds and her hands came away bloody. She scowled and looked back up at Lafayette, firing her gun at his black ass. Homie narrowed his eyes and blazed back on her ass mercilessly.

BOC! BOC!

Auntie's shoulders danced and she fell out fast, staring up at the sky and wheezing out of breath.

Lowering his warm weapon, Lafayette rushed over to Gar. He gripped his Main Man's hand, slicking his palm wet with blood in the process. Gar looked to Lafayette blinking his glassy eyes repeatedly, as if he was seeing a mirage and not his homeboy in the flesh.

"You're gonna be OK, my nigga, just hold on. Hold on!" Lafayette comforted him, caressing his crimson hand with his thumb.

Gar swallowed the lump of nervousness in his throat and nodded. Hearing Auntie's bawling in pain, he looked to her and then back to his homeboy. "Fi…finish…that bitch…"

Lafayette's face transformed into a mask of pure unadulterated hate, he laid his Main Man down and sped walked over to Auntie. Her eyes shifted to him as tears poured out of their corners. She went to say something but it was far too late.

BOC! BOC! BOC! BOC!

He filled her chest cavity with some hot shit, soaking that ass up. Auntie's head rolled to the left; her face now wore The Mask of Death. Lafayette ran over to Gar tucking his banger into the small of his back. He scooped his homie up into his arms and ran him over to the rental, the wounded man's limbs dangling along the way. Having placed him into the backseat, he slammed the door shut and jumped in behind the wheel, peeling off.

Chapter Fourteen

BOOM!

The double doors of the emergency room flew open as Gar was rushed through them on a gurney. Lafayette was gripping his hand and running beside him, entourage of hospital staff running along with them. The walls inside of the hall as well as the waxed floor appeared as flashes, with them moving so mothafucking fast.

"Sir, we've got it from here, you'll have to wait out in the lobby." one of the doctors told Lafayette. The hustler looked a mess. His eyes displayed worry and his clothes had splotches of blood on them.

Lafayette nodded in understanding and looked to Gar. "I'ma be waiting out front, my nigga. You don't worry about nothing, you gone be good! Don't wet it!" he held onto Gar's hand just a few seconds longer before letting go, his hand coming away with the blood that had dried on it. He stood out in the hall watching as the hospital staff wheeled Gar down the corridor and into the operation room, the doors closing behind them. Lafayette stood there for a while. He then took a deep breath and carried himself out of the emergency room, pushing through the doors that led him out into the lobby. All of the people in there seemed to be focused on the TV that was mounted high on the wall, flipping through magazines, on their cell phones or talking among one another. A couple of them glanced at Lafayette, seeing the brown stains on his clothing that was blood, but then they focused right back on what they were doing before he arrived. The hustler didn't pay them any mind. He entered the men's room and washed himself up as best as he could. Afterwards, he dried off his hands with the paper towels from the dispenser and balled them up; tossing them into the trash can on his way out. He then returned to the lobby where he sat down between two people and leaned back in his chair, shutting his eyes. He took a deep breath and allowed himself to relax a little bit.

TWO HOURS LATER

"How's he doing, doc?" Lafayette sprung to his feet when the doctor entered the lobby, setting the magazine he was reading aside on a nearby table.

The doctor took a deep breath before speaking.

"He's going to be fine, he's resting right now. Luckily you got him here as fast as you did. He lost a lot of blood. He almost didn't make it."

Lafayette sighed with relief and looked up to the ceiling thanking God. He then looked to the man that had a hand in saving his best friend's life, shaking his hand with both of his. "Thanks, doc, you think I can see 'em?"

"Nah, like I said, he's resting right now. How about you come by and see him tomorrow?"

"All right, cool, as long as my boy is good."

The doctor patted him on the shoulder and left the waiting room. Lafayette put his palms together and looked up at the ceiling. He thanked God Almighty once again for allowing his Main Man to remain on this earth.

***

Toting a black gym bag with L.A.P.D on it and a gold police shield, Montrice made her way down the steps of the basement. Once she reached the last step, she scanned her surroundings and approached the center of the room. She reached above her head and pulled a drawstring, restoring light to the underground dwelling. Next, she walked over to the refrigerator that sat up against the wall, sitting the gym bag down and pushing the refrigerator aside. Afterwards, she kneeled down and removed six red bricks from out of the wall, which left a hiding space behind.

Montrice looked inside of the hiding space and made sure it was clear. After seeing that it was, she unzipped her gym bag and pulled out the four cocaine blocks she'd stolen out of the evidence room. One by one, she placed the blocks of cocaine inside of the hiding space. Once she was done, she placed the red bricks back into their proper space and pushed the refrigerator back in place. She pulled the drawstring to turn off the light, and then headed back up the staircase, smiling evilly.

Lafayette didn't know what Montrice had in store for him, but by the time she was done with him he'd be regretting the day he'd ever put his hands on her.

***

When Lafayette pulled into the driveway of his home, the first thing he noticed was that the door was wide open. He reached underneath his seat and snatched his banger. He chambered a round into the head of his joint and hopped out of his whip, weapon held at his side. He left his door open because he didn't want to slam it and alert whoever was inside to his presence. He snuck his way up the steps and crept into the house, with caution. He proceeded towards his bedroom where he heard rummaging around. He stepped towards his bedroom and poked his head into the doorway. Inside he saw an assailant dressed in all black and rocking a ski-mask. The assailant was standing on his toes snatching Lafayette's amateur sex-tapes from the top of his closet and dropping them into a black garbage bag. The hustler could tell from the person's hourglass shape that they were a female, but he didn't give two fucks. She had thrown her life away the moment she decided to break into his home and steal his shit.

"Are you looking for something?" Lafayette's face balled up, gripping his steel tighter. His hand turned white at the knuckles he clutched it so firmly.

The assailant tensed and her hands shot up in the air. She slowly turned around to Lafayette, mad dogging him and smiling wickedly, holding up the middle finger. His eyes narrowed into slits and he tilted his head to the side, observantly. The next thing he felt was something crashing into the back of his skull and exploding, sending clay shards everywhere. Lafayette dropped to his knees and fell flat on his face, lying on the floor awkwardly. A second female dressed in all black, wearing a ski-mask and hooker boots stood over him, smacking the vase residue from her palms. She picked up his .9mm automatic and pointed it at the back of his dome. Her finger brushed against the trigger and something snatched her wrist back, pulling the banger up from his head.

"Bitch, we didn't come here to kill this mothafucka. We got what we want, now let's go." The other female assailant told her partner. She had the garbage bag of sex-tapes slung over her shoulder.

"Alright," She put the safety back on the banger and tossed it aside.

Lafayette pushed himself up from the floor on wobbly arms and legs. He groaned in pain and tried to shake off his dizzy spell. He'd gotten to one knee when he was kicked in the stomach by a hooker boot. When he doubled over and hugged his sides, a sharp blow to the temple sent his world spinning. He lay on his back and looked to his left. The last thing he saw were his black clad assailants running out of the front-door.

***

The sun shined through the openings of the blinds on Lafayette's face. He frowned and groaned in pain as he picked his head up from off the floor. He got to his feet rubbing the back of his head, where a lump had formed over night. He looked to the left and spotted his banger on the floor. He picked it up and checked its magazine. Seeing that it was partially full, he smacked it back into his weapon and stashed it on his waistline. Next, he journeyed into the kitchen, grabbed a Ziploc bag and filled it up with ice. He then held the ice bag to his dome and took a carton of Donald Duck orange juice to the head. A corner splashed out into his mouth and he licked his lips. He peeked inside of the carton and saw that it was empty. Afterwards, he smacked the carton on the kitchen counter and headed out of the door. He couldn't start his day off without breakfast and his favorite orange juice.

Lafayette hopped into the rental, fired up the engine and backed out of the driveway. On his way to the store, he decided to pull through the trap and see if his workers were on their shit that A.M, like they were supposed to be. Coasting down the block, he couldn't help seeing two dudes coming from the yard of his trap house. They both were flamed up. They stood out like a couple of flies in butter milk. Upon closer inspection, he identified the two dudes; they were a couple of young rowdy cats by the name of Krucial and Tragedy. Lafayette brought his rental to a stop beside Krucial and Tragedy as they stepped out onto the sidewalk. Krucial seemed happy to see him while Tragedy mad dogged him.

"Lafayette, just the man we've been looking for." Krucial threw up his hands and smiled with a chipped tooth. He made to approach the hustler's ride, but what he said next stopped him.

"Gimmie five feet, fam, I don't need you all up on my shit." Lafayette held up his hand, stopping the young knuckle-heads. His face was twisted into a scowl and he was gripping his .9mm automatic, which was lying on his lap.

"Damn, blood, it's like that? I knew you since I was knee high to a caterpillar." Krucial frowned, not feeling how Lafayette was coming at him. His brows furrowed and his nose scrunched up.

"That was a long time ago, Stanley. Shit changes, people change." Lafayette told him.

"Call me Krucial, man, I fucking hate my government."

Lafayette rolled his eyes and twisted his lips. "Anyway, Stanley, what chu want with me?"

"What's up with my man Gar? I heard he got jammed up last night." Krucial asked, ignoring what he'd been asked. He was heated that he insisted on calling him Stanley, but he held that animosity inside. He didn't want that mothafucka to know that he had struck a nerve.

"He'll be all right. I'm sliding through to see'em later on tonight."

Krucial nodded. "Man, I gotta go see my nigga."

"Like I was saying, 'what're y'all around here looking for me for?'"

"What chu mean, nigga? This our hood." A hostile Tragedy spoke for the first time. Seeing how hot that he was, Krucial stretched his arm across his chest to quiet him.

"Gangsta sent us through here, dawg. He wanted us to let chu know that he sees that business has picked up tremendously and he's going to have to raise your taxes." Krucial told him. "He wants five bands instead of the original two that y'all agreed upon."

"Yeah?" Lafayette raised an eyebrow.

"That's what he told me to tell you."

"Well, look here, *Stanley*, you tell Gangsta I'm not doing the five. You tell 'em I said take this funky ass two bands." He threw two thousand dollars at his chest and

they scattered everywhere upon impact, raining down on the street. "And the next time he thinks about raising my taxes, them people gone be lowering his casket." Krucial and Tragedy started in the hustler's direction, but when he rested his banger on the window pane they froze in their tracks. "What? I wish some fuck-niggaz would!" he laughed and sped off in the rental.

Lafayette thought that maybe he had went a little too far with his threatening Gangsta. The O.G had enough soldiers and enough guns to smash him and everyone he held dear. Though Lafayette had a little paper now, and a couple of cats he could pull together if some shit jumped off, the last thing he needed was another enemy to watch his back for.

Lafayette shrugged and said "Fuck it". He cranked up the music inside of his rental and continued on to his destination.

Chapter Fifteen

"This nigga hit me in the chest with some goddamn money, hunnit dolla bills scattered everywhere; made me feel like a chump. And I ain't nearly one of dem. My name stays ringing from the 20s to The Jungle. I'm official tissue." Krucial took the time to fire up a Newport and blew out a cloud of white smoke. "I'm telling you, Gangsta, this mothafucka Lafayette don't respect you or the set. We can't keep letting him get by on his brotha's good name. I got all of the love and respect in the world for 8-Ball, but it comes a time when niggaz have to draw a line." He picked a piece of lint off his crisp red thermal and brushed his shoulder off. "I think it's 'bout time we give that Tar Baby a spanking, nah what I'm saying?" Krucial took another pull from his Newport, smoke wafted around him. He narrowed his eyes.

The entire time Krucial was talking Gangsta had his back to him, clutching an old portrait of him and 8-Ball when they were younger. They were posted up in front of Gangsta's red Saab with the gold B.B rims. They were flamed up and throwing up their set. Gangsta took a deep breath and sat the portrait down. He turned around to Krucial and Tragedy. With a jeweled hand, he massaged his chin as he thought on the ordeal. Coming to a conclusion, he allowed his hand to drop to his side and gave his young wolves a nod.

Krucial smirked; all he needed was the green-light. He tapped Tragedy and they made their way for the door.

THAT NIGHT

Lafayette didn't know who the two broads were that broke into his house and stole his tapes, but he was sure he'd slid cock in both of them at some point and time. He was a hundred percent sure that they were at that meeting he had called all of his fuck-buddies so he could blackmail them for the grips he needed to start his operation. The women's voices seemed familiar to him but he couldn't quite place them. But the moment he did match the voices with the faces, those two broads were going to get some heat sent their way.

Lafayette pushed the thoughts of getting even with the two women that had snuffed him to the back of his brain. At the moment his mind was on Zay and La' Chat. They'd broken into his trap house, killed his people and stole his shit. He had a hard-on for them that you couldn't get from taking a little blue pill. Tonight was the night that he was going to make amends with the two man stickup crew. As soon as the sun had dipped below the skyline and allowed darkness to stake its claim, he threw open the door of his closet and started getting ready.

Lafayette got suited and booted in a ski-mask doubling as a black beanie, a black army jacket, matching cargo pants and combat boots. He stuck a pair of black leather gloves into the breast pocket of his army jacket and pulled an AR-15 equipped with an infrared laser, scope and silencer attachment from the back of the closet. He lugged the assault rifle up and braced the stock against his shoulder, aiming it at the lamp sitting on the nightstand. He then lowered the hefty weapon and stuffed two magazines inside of his army jacket's pocket. Homie then wrapped the AR-15 assault rifle in a blanket and headed out of his bedroom. Reaching for the knob of the front-door, he heard gunshots just outside his home.

***

Montrice pulled upon Lafayette's block and parked eight cars down and across the street from his house. Once she killed the engine, she grabbed her duffle bag with L.A.P.D emblazoned on it and sat it on her lap. She unzipped the duffle bag and took a peek at the four pretty White Bitches stored inside. She smiled fiendishly and zipped the duffle bag back up. She picked up the Slim Jim from the passenger seat, opened the door and hopped out. Hoodie over her head and a baseball cap pulled down tight over her brows, she made a beeline for Lafayette's rental.

Her plan was a simple one: plant the four blocks of cocaine into Lafayette's whip without him knowing, play the block until he left and call the police on him. With that much cocaine on him, Lafayette would never see the streets again. The act would be heinous and despicable, but she'd feel a lot better once she'd gotten her revenge on the hustler. All she could think about was getting even with him. The thought of it made her nipples hard.

Montrice was hunched over and creeping towards Lafayette's rental, when a man sprung before her from behind a parked car. She slowly rose to her feet and took in the full scope of the man. He was dressed in a ski-mask, black thermal, black jeans and black steel-toe boots. His hand shot to Montrice's face, extending a Taurus .9mm. She went to scream but her breath got caught in her throat. Her eyes traveled the length of the gun and settled on the menacing glare coming from the eye-holes of the ski-mask.

BOP! BOP!BOP! BOP! BOP!BOP!

The masked man sent a heat wave straight into Montrice's chest. Each slug hit her with an impact that forced her backwards until she collapsed on her back. She lay on the sidewalk, staring wide eyed into the sky and gasping for air. The masked man stood over her and pointed his weapon at her forehead.

BOP! BOP!

The masked man pushed Montrice into the next life and walked off into the night. The last thing that was heard was a car door slamming shut and the engine of a car as it sped away.

Officer down.

***

Lafayette stepped away from the front-door and peeked through the blinds. He saw people emerging from their homes to see what happened. Deciding that it was time that he headed on out, he opened the front-door as he stepped outside onto the porch, hustling down the steps. On his way down he saw a drove of people heading in the direction that the gunshots came from, but he didn't pay them any mind. He was on a mission. Besides, murder was a common thing in Lafayette's hood. Every other day someone was getting shot, stabbed or killed. The community had become desensitized to witnessing such violence. As far as they were concerned it came with the territory. It was what to be expected when coming up in the ghetto.

While everyone was distracted, Lafayette slipped behind the wheel of his rental and fired up its engine. He pulled off the block without anyone noticing his departure.

***

Lafayette cruised by Zay and La'Chat's crib just in time to see them stepping out onto the porch. By the time he'd doubled back, they were pulling away from the curb in an old turquoise blue Buick LeSabre with sun burns on its roof and hood. Lafayette followed them from a safe distance. Once they rolled out into traffic he kept a four car space between them. Though he'd missed the opportunity to lay them at their place of residence, he was hoping to catch up with them on the street and lay his murder game down. That hope was quickly thrown out of the window, being that it was 10 o'clock on a Saturday night and the streets were very much alive. Lafayette couldn't risk the chance of nailing them both and having someone see him, so he decided to lay on them until they reached their destination.

Lafayette followed Zay and La'Chat downtown into a dark area where there was an abundance of abandoned warehouses and factories. He killed the headlights of his rental and played the end of the block, watching what abandoned building Zay and La'Chat rolled into. Lafayette took refuge inside a ruined tenement across the street from the building the jacking couple

172

went into. He parked at the back of the building where no one would be able to make out his whip. He then pulled out the blanket that concealed his AR-15 and carried it up ten flights of steps. Once he made it to his destination, he went about his business of setting everything up.

***

When Zay and La' Chat pulled into the building a charcoal Avalanche truck sitting on chrome 26 inch rims was already present. A slender light skinned cat stood beside it with his arms folded across his chest. He rocked a Miami Dolphins snap-back backwards and propped upon his dome. He was dressed in all white and flossing icy jewels. He looked like he had just wrapped up the music video for his latest single.

"Don't even think about it?" Zay told La'Chat, seeing the thirsty look on her face.

"What?" she played dumb.

"We're not leaning on homie; I told you he's my folk's people."

La'Chat smirked and said, "You know me too well."

"Let's just make this drop and get up outta here." He pecked her lips. She then killed the engine and they hopped out of the Buick LeSabre.

"What's up? Easy," the light skinned cat outstretched his hand. Zay looked at his hand and allowed it to linger in the air before shaking it. He never uttered his name. "Aren't you gonna tell me your name?" his brows furrowed.

"No need. We aren't gonna be around long enough to get to know each other. You got that paper?" he asked in a no nonsense attitude.

"Yep," He looked to the Nike duffle bag Zay held clenched in his hand. "I take it my six birds are in there?" he pointed at the duffle bag. Again, Zay didn't utter a word. "Damn, homie, you don't have many people skills; anti-social like a mothafucka, G."

"I'm not big on talk. I came here to do business; not shoot the shit like a couple of old college buddies."

"Alright," Easy held the knapsack out for Zay, but La'Chat snatched it from his hand. "Ninety bands, it's all there." He said as he watched La'Chat peek inside of the duffle bag.

La'Chat nodded to her man, letting him know that the money was right. He then passed the Nike duffle bag to Easy. Homie sat the duffle bag on the hood of his Avalanche truck and unzipped it, peering inside. A smile stretched across his face when he saw all six of those lily White Girls snuggled neatly inside.

Easy grabbed the Nike duffle bag and approached Zay, cheesing like he was posing for a picture. He stopped before the big man, reaching inside of his jacket, he said, "You

174

played yourself mothafucka!" he made to pull his hand from out of his jacket and that's when all hell broke loose.

BOOM! BOOM! BOOM! BOOM!

***

Lafayette pulled his eye away from the scope of the AR-15 and looked beyond his weapon down at what just happened between Zay and Easy. He wore a shocked expression on his face; he couldn't believe what had just occurred. He placed his eye back into the scope. Then he placed his gloved finger to the trigger of the assault rifle and made to squeeze it. That's when the unthinkable unfolded before his eyes.

***

Easy staggered back into the side of his Avalanche truck and slid down to the ground, leaving a crimson smear behind. He looked off to the side, as dead as a doorknob with his hand still inside of his jacket. Zay lowered his smoking .44 Magnum revolver. He gave his lady the signal to stay put while he approached the dead man. He kneeled down to his victim and pulled his hand free from the inside of his jacket. He was clutching what looked like a wallet. Zay removed it from his hand and flipped it open. Inside there was a law enforcement shield. Zay closed his eyes and hung his head, massaging the bridge of his nose. He knew that he'd fucked up big time.

"Shit!" he cursed.

The loud spinning propellers coming from above stole Zay and La'Chat's attention. They looked up into the hollowed ceiling of the building and saw a police helicopter. Its light shined below and illuminated them, causing them to narrow their eyes into slits to avoid its bright ray. Right after there was a stampede. Dozens of men wearing blue windbreakers with D.E.A emblazoned on the back of them and bulletproof vest spilled into every passage of the building with his or her weapon drawn.

Zay's head whipped around to every passage inside of the building, watching as the place fill up with D.E.A agents.

"Fuck these pigs!" Zay donned a mask of hatred and pulled his .357 Magnum revolver. He now grasped both revolvers in his hands. "It's hammer time!"

"Baby, nooooo," La' Chat cried.

Zay looked to his woman and saw her eyes welling up with tears. Seeing her like that stung his heart. She was the only one in this world that he loved unconditionally. She had his back and he had hers. It tore him up inside to see her so vulnerable. He rarely saw this side of her. Her gangster matched his. He realized that she'd rather go to prison than to see him dead.

Zay looked around at all of the D.E.A agents, all of them had their weapons trained on them, ready to squeeze. Their

176

trigger-fingers were itching and poised to catch a couple of bodies. Zay sighed with frustration and tossed his Magnum revolvers aside. He and La'Chat got down to their knees with their hands behind their heads. As a couple of agents moved in to cuff them, they stared into one another's eyes. She mouthed "I love you" and he mouthed it back, grinning.

***

Lafayette cursed and punched the wall when he saw the D.E.A agents swarm in and arrest Zay and La'Chat. Now his six birds were gone and he would never get his revenge. Realizing this, the hustler pulled his AR-15 out of the window and sat up against the wall. He then lit up a blunt of Kush seeing how he wasn't going anywhere for a while. He sat up and listened to all of the activity across the street inside of the other building.

***

"You're finished, pal. Washed up." The D.E.A agent told Zay as he handcuffed his wrists behind his back. The muscle bound bandit wasn't paying him any mind though. Nah, he was focused on his crying wife, who was also being hand-cuffed. As the agent went on talking shit about how Zay and his wife were never going to see the light of day again, homie kept right on speaking to his lady.

"I love you, La' Chat." He said, looking her straight in her eyes and grinning.

"I love you too, bae. You're the man of my dreams and my reality." This was the last thing that she said to him before she was placed into the backseat of an unmarked car, door slamming shut on her. She quickly scooted to the window of the vehicle and looked out at her man; he'd just been placed in the back of an unmarked car as well. They stared out at one another as their respective vehicles were started up. The cars pulled off, with the couples communicating through the windows. They'd use their hot breaths to fog up the glass and their noses to write a message in it.

I have no regrets, I'd live this life with you all over again, La' Chat wrote on the fogged up window.

So would I, Zay wrote back to her in his fogged up window.

Once the white smear from his breath disappeared from off of the window, he fogged it up again. He then wrote his name and her name, with the infinity symbol in between them. When she seen this she broke down sobbing. She then sniffled and fought back her tears, writing back to him, Forever. He nodded to her, letting her know that's what he meant, her and him forever.

Zay let his forehead fall against the window and submitted to his emotions, breaking down crying. His shoulders shudder and tears flooded his cheeks, he turned his face away from the window so his wife wouldn't see him in this state. She reacted the same way that he did, turning her face away from the window. At that moment the respective unmarked cars departed from one another, one trailing after the other.

Zay and La'Chat drifted off to sleep crying. When they finally awoke, they'd be ready to face the consequences for their actions.

Chapter Sixteen

Once the D.E.A agents were gone, Lafayette wrapped his AR-15 back into the blanket and stuffed it into the trunk of his rental. He pulled his banger off his hip and slid over into the driver seat. He laid his joint on the passenger seat and turned the key in the ignition; the engine came back to life and he rolled out.

Lafayette coasted through the streets, gripping the steering-wheel with one hand. He turned the radio on and 50 cent's *I'm supposed to die tonight* came ripping through the air. He pulled the half smoked L from behind his ear and slipped it between his lips. Next, he pressed the cigarette lighter in and a moment later it popped out. Afterwards, he pulled the cigarette-lighter out and went to light up the L, when he accidentally dropped it on the floor. He leaned forward to pick it back up and the passenger side window's glass imploded, followed by the driver side window's glass. Lafayette's slowly lifted his head up and peered out of the passenger side window. Beyond it he saw Krucial steering the wheel of a Jeep Cherokee Sport. His face was twisted into a mean mug and his gloved hand was extended out of the window, clutching a

Calico M950. He pulled the trigger of his weapon and sent fire in Lafayette's direction, blowing holes through his passenger side door. The hustler ducked and snatched his thang off the passenger seat. He waited for a second, and then came back up, sending some hot shit back at Krucial.

BLOC! BLOC!

"Aghhhh!!!" a yelp came from within the Jeep Cherokee.

Lafayette thought he'd hit his target, but it was Tragedy that caught one in the neck. He was leaning against the passenger side window holding his bleeding neck, clenching his jaws in excruciating pain and squeezing his eyes shut. A worried Krucial looked to his comrade. It was that split second that gave his enemy all the time he needed to react. Lafayette leaned over into the passenger seat and pointed his thang out of the window.

BLOC! BLOC! BLOC! BLOC!

Krucial howled in pain. A bullet whizzed through his wrist and caused him to drop his Calico into the street, sending it tumbling. Another one met his jaw, a third lodged into his shoulder, and in his rib cage. His face twisted feeling the fire engulfing the left side of his body. He closed his eyes tightly trying to fight back the pain, biting down on his bottom lip. When he peeled them back open, he was about to crash into a telephone pole. The nigga'z eyes lit up and he said 'Oh shit.'

182

He quickly sat up turning the steering-wheel back on course, but Lafayette slammed his whip into the side of his, sending the Cherokee spiraling out of control.

URRRRRRK!

CRAAAAAASH!

The Cherokee crashed into a white brick wall. Bricks scattered everywhere; some of them slammed into the truck's windshield and cracked it into a spider's cobweb. Krucial lay slumped in his seat with crimson streams running down his face. He looked over to Tragedy whose head was lying against the dashboard, oozing blood. He grabbed the back of his collar and pulled him back into the passenger seat, his head bumping off of the headrest. He was cockeyed and his jaw was slackened. His time on earth had expired.

SCREEEEEECH!

Krucial looked to his left and saw Lafayette's rental halting to a stop. He then saw the driver side door swing open and his enemy hurriedly hopping out, speed walking in his direction. Krucial's heart quickened, pummeling his chest bone. He looked back over to Tragedy and saw that his hand was still clutching his P89. He reached over Tragedy trying to grasp the P89 in his hand. Using the tips of his fingers, he was able to pull the P89 into his palm and curl his fingers around its handle. He gripped it tightly and brought it around.

BLOC! BLOC! BLOC!

Krucial's dome exploded and bloody chunks of brain dropped into Tragedy's lap.

"Bitch ass niggaz!" Lafayette snarled. "The next time you get at a gangsta, come correct!" he leaned over into the Cherokee and popped one more slug into Tragedy's crown before hustling back to his rental and peeling off.

Back inside of the rental, Lafayette slipped his half smoked L back between his lips. He pushed the cigarette-lighter back into its slot so that it could heat up, and that's when he noticed that he had been shot in the shoulder.

"Shit!" he cursed.

There was no way he was going to a hospital. The police would be notified that he had been shot and cops would be crawling all over the place. They'd quickly piece together the puzzle and figure that he had something to do with the two bodies he just slumped. He would have to patch himself up and see if Victoria could have someone check him out later.

Lafayette drove into the driveway of his house and stashed his rental inside of the garage. Afterwards, he went inside and changed clothes. Once he was dressed, he hopped into his Buick Regal and drove over to a 24 hour Rite Aid on Vermont and 4th avenue. He gathered up everything he thought he may need to treat his wound and stood on line to pay for his items.

Looking over his shoulder, he saw a police officer opening the door of one of the refrigerators to get a cold beverage. When he turned back around the last customer had just stepped away, so he approached the counter and sat his items down.

"Will that be all?" the cashier asked.

"Hold up." Lafayette looked to the candy rack. He saw a box of Tootsie Roll pops all the way at the bottom of the rack. He reached down into the box to grasp a cherry one and that's when he heard it.

"Freeze!" he looked over his shoulder and saw the police officer with his gun pointed at him. His forehead wrinkled and his heart skipped a beat. The first thing he thought was someone had seen him when he blasted on Krucial and Tragedy. But that couldn't have been, because he was masked up when he gave them the business. He chalked it up to a case of mistaken identity. "Slowly place your hands behind your head and get down on your knees!" the police officer ordered. Lafayette did as he was told. The police officer approached him cautiously, keeping his gun on him. One hand held the gun on Lafayette while the other reached for his hip. Lafayette's eyes shot to their corners and saw the police officer's hand pull his .9mm banger free. Right then, he closed his eyes and shook his head, cursing himself. He had gotten so accustomed to carrying his joint that it had become a part of him.

Sometimes he'd forget that it was there on his hip. He didn't even notice that he still had it on him when he dipped inside of the house to change his clothes.

When the police officer snapped the handcuffs around Lafayette's wrists he knew that he was fucked with a capital F. His banger had Krucial and Tragedy's bodies on it. The thought of life imprisonment came up in his thoughts and he felt sick. He literally felt like throwing up. The police officer pulled him to his feet and escorted him out of Rite Aid, holding his head down. He knew that he'd probably never see the streets again.

Chapter Seventeen

Victoria sat behind her desk inside of her study, staring at a photograph of her and Shameek while sipping a glass of Brandy. Her eyes began to well up with tears and cloud her vision as she reminisced about the good times they'd shared. For as hard as she acted, she was still a woman. Therefore she was forever a slave to her emotions, though she did tend to think more with her head than her heart. The tears flooded Victoria's eyes and spilled down her cheeks. Her vision became coated with a red haze of anger and her face contorted into something monstrous.

"Fuck him! Fuck'em both!" she said of her late husband and his side chick, Gemma. She smacked the photograph down on the desk and poured herself another glass of Brandy. Next, she snatched her desk's drawer open, removed a box of matches and took out a match stick. She then swept the match across the black strip at the end of the box and a reddish orange flame was born, smoke wafting from it. She tossed the match on the soaked photograph and it went up in flames quickly.

Victoria lit up a joint and wiped her tear slicked face with the back of her hand sniffling. She watched the flames engulf the photograph and curl the ends of it. The photograph had almost been disintegrated when someone rapped on the door. Victoria smacked away the flames of the burning photograph and brushed its burnt ashes into a waste basket. She sat the waste basket aside, fixed herself up in a palm sized mirror and cleared her throat.

"Come in." she said to whoever was on the other side of the door. Afterwards, she placed the mirror inside of her desk drawer and pushed it shut.

Ren came through the door sniffing around. He was dressed in all black and rocking boots.

"It's OK, Ren. Come inside." She waved him inside of her study.

Ren hesitantly stepped inside and closed the door behind him.

"What's burning?" he asked, forehead wrinkling.

"It must be coming from outside. Close the window." Ren closed the window and sat down before Victoria at her desk, crossing his legs like the gangster and gentleman that he was. He then cleared his throat with his fist to his mouth and clasped his hands in his lap.

"The cop…She's gone off to a better place." Ren cut his throat with the side of his hand, bringing it around his neck.

Lafayette gave Victoria the information she needed to take care of Montrice. He led Victoria to believe that she was pressuring him to set her up and if he didn't she'd make it so that he'd never see sunlight again. With that in mind, Victoria gave Ren the go ahead to turn Montrice's lights out. See, Lafayette didn't want anything to do with Montrice or the baby. He'd been dealing with her for quite some time so he knew her like the back of his hand. After what went down between him and her the other day, Lafayette was sure that she'd hatch something that would guarantee him a funeral or life behind bars. He wasn't having it either way so he pressed a button that would end her existence.

***

Lafayette was arrested and booked on an unlawful possession of a firearm charge. It was two o'clock into Sunday morning, which meant he'd see a judge Monday. He needed someone there to pay his bail as soon as his arraignment was over so he could get the fuck out of Los Angeles. If he was still in custody once they'd run the ballistics on his banger he'd be looking at a long stay in County jail, fighting a couple of murder beefs.

Lafayette picked up the phone and punched in the number of the only person that could pull his ass out of the fire. He held the telephone to his ear and listened as the phone rang, closing his eyes tightly, he prayed someone picked up.

***

Victoria sat a glass down beside hers and picked up the bottle of Brandy. "Have a drink with me." She said to Ren. Before he'd answered she was filling two glasses. She picked up her glass and he picked up his glass. "Salute," They clinked their glasses together and took a sip. The telephone rang and she snatched it up. "Hello! Jail? What happened? OK. I'll send someone to make the…"

BOOM!

An explosion rocked the mansion with the strength of an earthquake.

"What the hell was that?" Ren shot to his feet and drew his banger, ready to give a bitch ass nigga a tombstone.

Victoria looked to the security screen on her desk and saw a drove of men carrying machine-guns spilling through the doorway of her mansion. Once her eyes sent the information to her brain what was happening, her heart thundered inside of her chest. Her eyes bulged and she gasped.

"Shit! We're under attack!" Victoria dropped the telephone to the floor and grabbed her cell phone. Afterwards, she

190

called the only person that she could think of. They didn't pick up so she left them a message. Next, she unzipped her jeans and stuffed it inside of her pussy. She rushed over to her book shelf and pulled on a thick burgundy book. Something clicked and the opposite side of the shelf slid back. A few Kevlar bulletproof vests and an arsenal of weapons were exposed. She grabbed two bulletproof vests, strapping one to her body and throwing one to Ren. Next, she then snatched up two AK-47s with drums, keeping one for herself and tossing one over to Ren. At the same time they checked the banana clips then smacked them back in, cocking the hammers on their deadly weapons and heading for the door. Ren reached for the door-knob.

Boom!

The door was blown off by an explosion, fire and black smoke filled the study. Victoria lay on her back gagging and coughing on smoke while Ren lay under the door. He was missing an arm and his left leg had been stripped down to the bone. They both narrowed their eyes into slits trying to see through the smoke and debris. The smoke cleared revealing the man behind all of the mayhem. He was a brown skinned man of average height with a protruding gut. He had a nest of dark hair and thick a beard. The hair on his face made him look wolf like. The shades that he was wearing showed the fires that were scattering throughout the study's floor.

The brown skinned man lumbered forth wearing a cast and clutching an M-16. The further he walked into the study the more of him came into view until all of him was shown. He smiled wickedly and his evil eyes bore into Victoria's. She gritted her teeth and then spat at his boots.

"Diablo." she spoke his name.

Seeing Diablo moving in on his boss, Ren reached for his AK-47 with his one good hand. Even as a cripple he was going to give his all to save his boss's life, it was his duty. He wrapped his hand around the handle of the choppa and swung it around.

Blaaaaaaaaaaaaaaaaaaaat!

Diablo walked past Ren. Without even looking, he pointed his M-16 at him and pulled the trigger. The missile shaped bullets blew Ren's face off, stripping it down to the bloody skeletal bone structure of his skull. Diablo's henchmen poured inside of the study and surrounded Victoria. At Diablo's orders they snatched Victoria up by her arms and held her up against the wall. She mad dogged Diablo with a viciousness that would cause you to think that she'd bare her teeth and tear his throat out of his neck.

***

BLAAAAAAAAAAAAAT!

The sound of an automatic weapon ripping through the air from the other side of the telephone startled Lafayette.

"Victoria! Victoria! Victoriaaaa," Lafayette yelled into the telephone as he clutched it tightly to his ear.

"Time's up, bruh," an African American sheriff's deputy took the telephone from Lafayette's hand and hung it up. He then escorted him back to the holding cell. Lafayette sat on the bottom bunk leaning forward with his elbows on his knees and his hands clasped. Thoughts ripped through his mental about Victoria, he wondered who hit her mansion. He wasn't a hundred percent sure, but he'd bet his money on Diablo. He and a handful of his soldiers were the only ones that didn't get hit when Victoria brought it to The Sanchez Cartel. Lafayette gripped his head and brought his hands down his face. He then blew hard and massaged his chin, thinking. If Victoria's crib did get hit then more than likely she and Ren were dead. If that was so then he was fucked. He would definitely be brought up on murder charges before he could make bail.

Damn, Lafayette thought to himself. Just as the thought entered his brain the lights inside of the cell were turned off.

***

Jason sat on the living room couch twisting his platinum wedding band around his finger. It was 3 o'clock in the morning and Montrice hadn't made it home yet. His gut told him that she was more than likely out fucking around, which made him wish he wouldn't have cancelled the contract he'd put out on her. For as heated as he was he couldn't bring himself to go along with having her murdered. Somehow he'd convinced himself that their marriage could work. He was hoping to put Montrice's shady past behind him and give their union one last shot. He knew he would get an earful from his mother which is why he wasn't going to tell her. When the baby was born he or she would get his last name and all of this would be like it had never happened. He couldn't wait for Montrice to get back home so they could talk things over. They just really needed to sit down, chop it up and see where one another's head was.

Jason picked up the cordless telephone to place a call to Montrice when the door bell chimed. He sat the cordless phone back on the nightstand and went down the staircase. He glanced through the peephole and saw two detectives on his front porch. His forehead wrinkled wondering what the two men were doing at his house at this hour. Thinking nothing of it, he unchained, unlocked and snatched the door open.

"Are you Jason Shakur?" The Latin Detective asked. He nodded yes. "Sorry to disturb you at this hour, Mr. Shakur. I'm Detective Francisco Rivera and this is my partner Detective Dawayne Bishop." He flashed his badge before sticking it back inside of his overcoat. "We're here about your wife, Officer Montrice Shakur."

"Is she OK?" Jason adjusted his glasses, looking between the two detectives.

Detective Rivera took a deep breath and exhaled. "You mind if we come inside for a moment?"

Jason opened the door wider and stepped aside, leaving a clear path for the two detectives to enter.

Chapter Eighteen

Four days later

Lafayette's bail had been set and he was bussed to the County jail. Now he had enough money to post his bail, his only problem was finding someone that he trusted enough to get his stash and bail him out. There wasn't anyone that he could think of that he could count on like that, so he knew he'd be a sitting duck until he could advise some other plan to spring him free from The Belly of the Beast. He was sure that the ballistics had come back on by now, and if they hadn't they would be pretty soon. If that happened, his only way out of his situation would be to escape, and that wouldn't be an easy feat, even with his connections.

Not only did he have the murders on his gun hanging over his head, but the possibility of him getting murdered behind the wall weighed on his shoulders as well. See, as soon as he entered behind the barbed wire walls some Mexican cats were on him like flies on shit. They tried to kill him when he went to go shower but he was able to fend them off. He'd gotten stabbed in the arm but it wasn't life threatening. Being the G that he was he wanted to go back to general population, but those white folks weren't having that. Nah, they put his black ass in involuntary protective custody.

Lafayette had a lot of alone time, so he kept himself busy with his contraband cell phone. If he wasn't jacking off to porn then he was watching movies. One night after making an important call, he lay back in his bunk with his hands steepled behind his head. He found his eyes growing heavier and heavier with each minute that passed by until they eventually shut. The nigga was asleep when the door of his cell was unlocked and a correctional officer stepped inside.

***

Lafayette's eyes fluttered open. His vision was blurry, but it came back into focus after a while. He gave himself the once over, seeing that he was bound to a chair by heavy silver chains. Although he was restrained, it didn't stop him from trying to get loose. His struggling caused the chair that he was perched in to slide slightly across the floor. He attempted this for a while and all it did was tire him, leaving him breathing hard. His chest inflated and deflated, as he inhaled and ex-haled, looking about. He was inside of the shower room, which was dimly lit. He looked around for someone or some-thing that would lead him to his salvation, but there wasn't anyone or anything in sight. A moment later, he heard foot-steps come from his left. When he looked a correctional officer came to a stop inside of the doorway, standing off to the side. He looked in at the mothafucka bound to the chair and then folded his arms across his chest, leaning up against the doorway. Soon after there was whistling, drawing closer and closer. Then there was the sound of something metal being drug on the cement floor. The noise stopped at the door way. There was the silhouette of a short man carrying something long and curved at its end. He patted the C.O on the arm and stepped inside of the shower room, walking in Lafayette's direction. The closer he got to the hustler, the more he began to fill out under the dim lighting that the shower room provided. The short man suddenly stopped before Lafayette. His face was partially hidden by the darkness of the room so the hustler peered closer to identify him. When recognition ripped through his brain, he had to blink a few times to be sure of who was standing before him.

"Lil…Lil…Lil…" he stammered.

"Lil Man, alive and in the mothafucking flesh," The little nigga smiled wickedly and tapped the pipe in his palm.

***

Gar lay in his hospital bed in darkness, eyelids shut, mouth forming a straight line. The only thing that could be heard was the noises that the medical machinery made, as they worked to keep him alive. Suddenly, his eyelids and his fingers twitched.

***

Loon stepped to the commode and unzipped his jeans, pulling out his meat. He parted his legs and tilted his head back. A relieved expression came across his face as he pissed into the toilet bowl. Once he was done, he gave his limp dick to shakes before putting it back inside of its denim prison and zipping back up. Flushing, he walked to the porcelain sink and turned on the water. Lathering his hands, he held them under the flowing water, occasionally glancing at his appearance in the medicine cabinet mirror. His eyebrows arched and his nose crinkled, seeing all of the damage that had been done to him due to Gar beating him with his gun.

Loon's face was twice its size and his left eye was swollen shut. He had black and blue bruising underneath both eyes and six cuts on his face. His leg was also in a cast having been shot twice. Seeing himself in his current state made him mad as a mothafucka. He had business in the streets that he needed to attend to, but, fuck that; it could take the backseat to him getting his revenge. He didn't know where that nigga Gar was laid up, but he knew one thing, he was going to find his ass and kill him.

CRACK!

He slammed his fist into the mirror and it cracked into a spider's cobweb. When he drew his fist back it had small cuts on it from the assault. He looked down into the sink and saw pieces of broken glass that twinkled like diamonds, sprinkled with dots of blood. Loon snatched a washcloth from off of the rack where it was laying on a towel. He wrapped the washcloth around his fist and used his teeth to tie it up. Afterwards, he left the bathroom and entered his master bedroom, opening the closet door. He pulled the drawstring and the light bulb inside of the closet gave the space light. Parting his clothes that were hanging on the rack, he exposed the AK-47 lying up against the wall. He snatched the deadly weapon up and checked the banana clip, that bitch was fully loaded so he smacked it back in. Holding the assault rifle down at his side in one hand, he limped out of the closet and entered the hallway. Pulling out his cellular, he called up the nigga he had business with that night.

"'Sup, my nigga? Nah, homie, I'ma have to get up witchu later on, some shit came up. Cool." He hung up and stuck the cell phone into his pocket. When he came out the backdoor, he headed over to his old school Buick Regal and slid in behind the wheel, cranking that thang up. The headlights came on and smoke wafted from the exhaust pipes. Putting the vehicle into drive, he pulled off and drove down his driveway. He cruised through the streets wearing a scowl, the street lights flashing on and off of his face. He took the time to fire up a half smoked blunt that was lying inside of the ashtray. After he sucked on the end of it, he blew out a big cloud of smoke.

To Be Concluded…

The Last Real Nigga Alive 3

AVAILABLE NOW BY TRANAY ADAMS

The Devil Wears Timbs 1-5

Bury Me A G 1-3

Tyson's Treasure 1-2

Treasure's Pain

A South Central Love Affair

Me And My Hittas 1- 6

The Last Real Nigga Alive 1-3

Fangeance

Fearless

COMING SOON BY TRANAY ADAMS

The Devil Wears Timbs 6: Just Like Daddy

A Hood Nigga's Blues

Bloody Knuckles

Billy Bad Ass